REVENGE
OF THE
GREEN
BANANA

REVENGE OF THE GREEN BANANA

Jim Murphy

CLARION BOOKS

HOUGHTON MIFFLIN HARCOURT

BOSTON   NEW YORK

Clarion Books

3 Park Avenue

New York, New York 10016

Copyright © 2017 by Jim Murphy

All rights reserved. For information about permission to reproduce selections

from this book, write to trade.permissions@hmhco.com or to

Permissions, Houghton Mifflin Harcourt Publishing Company,

3 Park Avenue, 19th Floor, New York, New York 10016.

Clarion Books is an imprint of Houghton Mifflin Harcourt Publishing Company.

www.hmhco.com

The text was set in Carre Noir Std.

LIBRARY OF CONGRESS CATALOGING-IN-PUBLICATION DATA

Names: Murphy, Jim, 1947–author.

Title: Revenge of the green banana / Jim Murphy.

Description: Boston ; New York : Clarion Books, Houghton Mifflin Harcourt,

[2017] | Summary: Jimmy Murphy starts sixth grade determined to be a

better student and impress the beautiful Kathy Guenther,

but Sister Angelica has him and his friends

pegged as troublemakers and they may just prove her right.

Identifiers: LCCN 2015051335 | ISBN 9780544786776 (hardback)

Subjects: | CYAC: Catholic schools—Fiction. | Schools—Fiction.

| Nuns—Fiction. | Friendship—Fiction. | Behavior—Fiction. | Practical

jokes—Fiction. | Humorous stories. | BISAC: JUVENILE FICTION / School &

Education. | Juvenile Fiction / Humorous Stories. | Juvenile Fiction/

Social Issues / Friendship.

Classification: LCC PZ7.M9535 Rev 2017 | DDC [Fic]—dc23

LC record available at https://lccn.loc.gov/2015051335

Manufactured in the United States of America

DOC 10 9 8 7 6 5 4 3 2 1

4500630049

*To all the teachers at St. Stephen's, each and every one.
I want to apologize for what I did and thank you
for putting up with my antics for so many years.
I entered St. Stephen's as one sort of kid
and left as an entirely different one.*

Warning: Everything in this book is absolutely true and actually happened, and no names have been changed to protect the identity of the innocent or the guilty.* Especially the guilty. And let me tell you, when I went to St. Stephen's Elementary School in Kearny, New Jersey, way back somewhere in the 1950s, there were a lot of guilty people wandering the halls who should have been in leg irons and handcuffs. Some wore street clothes and posed as students, while others were draped in long black flowing robes and claimed to be Sisters of Charity. So remember, if you see your name in here, you've been warned. Or as Philip might say, *Caveat emptor.*

---

* Okay, I have to make a confession. The truth is that just about every name in this book is real, but not *every* every one is, if you get my drift. But, after all, this is a novel, which means it's fiction, which means that some stuff is made up. In a way, everyone who writes a novel is a liar in big and small ways (but that's a subject you should take up with your language arts teacher if you really want to know the truth).

Contents

1
Where to Start?

WHERE TO START a story is the hardest part of starting it. I could write about the first day of every year I went to St. Stephen's, because each one was strange and awful. Awful in a different way every time, of course. For instance, I was probably the only kid ever who was suspended on his first day in kindergarten *even before I actually stepped foot inside the school!* No kidding.

How did I manage that? I was on line with all the other kindergartners, marching into school for the very first time. Before I got to the door, I spotted a bunch of kids down the sidewalk a ways, pushing my older brother, Jerry, around and bullying him. So I charged out of line and tackled one of the kids hard enough to knock him to the ground. A second later a very big nun yanked me to my feet and called for the principal, Sister Rose Mary. This was not, as you might imagine, the very best first impression.

Oh, and on the first day of second grade I organized a contest to see who could spit the farthest. I launched a spectacular gob just as Sister Benedicta approached to demand what I was up to. The gob landed on some kid's shoe, and I landed in Sister Rose Mary's office.

And then there was this other time . . .

Okay, I need to stop before I use up too much space without actually, you know, starting my story. I decided to begin with the first day of sixth grade.

My class was marched into a classroom on the second floor of the old building, all sixty-two of us. You heard me right. Sixty-two in one classroom. St. Stephen's was a private school and didn't have to follow the state rules about class size. We walked in, girls in front, boys behind them, in a long line according to height. Which meant I was toward the back of the line, but not quite at the end, since Iggy and Tom-Tom and Squints were taller than me. Well, Iggy's hair was taller than mine, so he was always just behind me.

Normally, I scurried to the back of the room and found a seat near the corner. That's the best place to hide from an annoying nun's radar. Today I went to the fifth row and found a seat near the teacher's desk and not far from Kathy Gathers's. I put my new pencil box on the desk and sat up tall, back straight, eyes forward.

"Murph. Murph. We're back here." That was Vero, trying to get me to grab the seat next to him in the back. Way far away from the teacher. "Come on, before—"

"Master Vero," said a voice as brittle as ice. A very tall nun swept into the room, her black robe billowing and flapping behind her. Most nuns have a slow, floating walk, but this one seemed to fly from the door to her desk.

She didn't look at Vero until she came to an abrupt, almost angry stop. Then she turned with a no-nonsense scowl on her face and stared at him hard. Her stare looked extra severe and annoyed because her face was crammed into the starched white rectangular frame her veil was attached to. My dad had told me the cardboard frame was called a coif, and he knew that because one of his cousins from the Old Country had been a nun. Whatever, the frame was so tight, her face seemed to be desperately trying to escape.

She was new to the school, and I wondered how

she knew who Vero was. She added, "I could hear your voice out in the hall."

"Yes, Sister," Vero said, scrambling to his feet. You never answered a nun in class without scrambling to your feet and snapping to attention. "I mean, no, Sister. I mean, I'm sorry, Sister. I just wanted to tell——"

"Tell him at lunch. But in a lower voice." She paused for a long moment, enough time for me to notice the age lines around her eyes. The room was so quiet I thought I could hear Vero sweating. "Have I made myself clear, Master Vero?"

"Ah, yes, Sister," Vero said in a fading voice.

There was another long silence as the nun looked at Vero as if he were a smelly bottom-feeding fish caught in her net. "You may sit down now."

"Thank you, Sister." Vero sat down so hard that his metal desk-chair scraped along the floor. I could imagine him sliding down in his seat, trying to disappear.

"All right, class." The nun turned and wrote the date on the blackboard in large, neat letters: September 8, 1958. Then below that, in much fancier letters, she wrote her name: *Sister Angelica Rose*. "Now you know my name. And I know some of your names." She glanced quickly in Vero's direction, but didn't explain how she came to know his name. Some sort of nun magic, I supposed. "But there are a number of faces I don't know, so we might as well learn everyone's name together."

"Yes, Sister Angelica," the class said as one.

"We'll start to my left." Sister Angelica pointed a long, thin finger at Erin O'Connor. "Please tell us your name and what you did this summer."

"Yes, Sister." Erin popped to her feet and snapped to attention so hard that her back curved in what must have been a painful arch, her head tilted so far back she was staring at the ceiling. "My name is Erin Margaret Patricia O'Connor—"

"*Erin go Bragh*," Philip whispered from somewhere far behind me. Philip stuttered and had a lisp, so when he talked in English, he generally sprayed the audience. He'd discovered long ago that if he said short phrases in a foreign language, they somehow came out easily. And dry. (Oh, and if you want to know what he was really saying, go to page 213.)

"Erin go bra-less," Vero replied. Both Philip and Vero thought Erin was the prettiest girl in the two sixth-grade classes, but they clearly had different ways of expressing their affection.

". . . but I like the name Margaret better than Erin,

so my friends call me Maggy," Erin went on, "but my brother calls me Mags, but I don't much like it, but he doesn't listen to me—"

"Erin, dear." Sister Angelica interrupted her gently. If a teacher was really annoyed at someone, she'd address that person as Miss or Master So-and-so. Using Erin's first name meant that Erin was safe. "I mean Margaret. Your name will do for now." Some kids giggled a little, but not many. Most kids liked Erin, no matter what they called her, and didn't want to make her feel bad by laughing at her. "Remember, Margaret, brevity is the soul of wit."

"Ah, yes, Sister."

"And what did you do this summer?"

"Nothing, Sister." There were more giggles. Our whole class had been together since kindergarten, and we knew that Erin always explained everything in endless detail. She could string together more words with one tiny breath than anyone. Only I guess she was thinking about the brevity-wit thing and worrying that if she said anything more, it would bother Sister Angelica.

"Nothing? Even if you didn't go on a family vacation, you must have done something. Correct?"

"No, Sister. I mean, yes, Sister." Erin inhaled

deeply, and her eyes bulged just a little. She was like a balloon about to pop. Then in a whoosh she explained, "You see, Sister, my father lost his job at Gary Plastics in the spring, but it wasn't his fault. But he couldn't find another job, but then my mother found out she was, um, you know, going to have another baby, but—"

Erin was off to the races, and all Sister Angelica could do was look at her and blink several times. She had, after all, sort of pushed for an answer. And now she was getting it.

Erin was pretty. Long red hair, bright green eyes, and more freckles on her face than stars in the sky. But I thought Kathy Gathers was the absolute prettiest girl ever. Golden blond hair, amazing periwinkle blue eyes, and a killer smile. She was why I was sitting so dangerously close to the teacher's desk this year, pencil box on my desk filled with neatly sharpened #2 pencils, ready for a new school year. And a new beginning.

On the last day of fifth grade, about one minute before dismissal, Sister Anita had made an announcement. Most of us groaned and started to squirm, since all nun announcements last at least a half-hour and we wanted to be out of there and officially on summer vacation. But I started to pay attention when she said that sixth grade would be the most important grade of all in our education. That it would determine where we would go to high school and college, where we would get jobs, where we would live with our future families. I hoped Kathy would be in my future family. "Think of sixth grade as a chance to change, a chance to make a new beginning," she'd said.

She said more, but my brain was churning over the part about a new beginning. Starting fresh sounded great to me. A lifesaver, even. I was hands down the worst student in our grade, if not in the whole school. Definitely not one of the good-smart kids — you know, the ones who never got in trouble and always got good grades. Sixth grade might be a good time to actually force my brain to stop thinking about a thousand different things long enough to study a little and maybe get better grades. It would certainly make my parents happy, but what I really wanted was to make Kathy happy. Especially after what had happened in fifth grade.

Sometime that year, I decided I liked Kathy Gathers so much I had to get her attention. So I wrote a short story on yellow lined paper and showed it to the kid next to me, who showed it to the kid on the other side of him. They seemed to like it. My plan was that eventually it would get to Kathy, and she would really like it — and me, too. And Kathy did read it, because the next thing I knew, she and her mother were knocking on the front door of my house.

You see, the story was about a girl named, well, Kathy Gathers, who was so fat that she couldn't fit through regular-size door openings. She tried to lose weight, but she just couldn't stop stuffing her face with jelly doughnuts, potato chips, black and white cookies, and pistachio nuts. I added pistachio nuts because I thought they sounded exotic.

Turned out that saying a girl is fat is a great way to get her attention, but not a great way to get her to like you. You can take my word for that. The meeting between her mother and my mother went as well as you might expect. After my mother heard about what I'd written, she looked at me strangely. She wasn't happy that I had said Kathy was so fat she got stuck in a doorway and had to have ten kids push her through. She scolded me — "How in heaven's name could you even do such a thing and not know it would hurt Kathy's feelings?" And she made me apologize right away. But there was more to that look Mom gave me — a surprised expression that seemed positive

—maybe because I wasn't noted for writing two-page book reports or short assignments or anything else, let alone an actual story with a beginning, middle, and end. After apologizing, I promised never to write another story about Kathy, though I really wanted to say *But I love you and think you're the prettiest girl in the class. In the world! And you're really not fat, and*—

But now I was in sixth grade, the land of new beginnings. And if I could improve my grades a little, maybe I could also improve things with Kathy. That was possible, I guessed. I mean, hope is a good thing, and . . .

"Next!" That icy, sharp voice seemed to shout. In a tone that made it clear this wasn't the first time the command had been given.

Seems that while I was daydreaming about new beginnings, the name and vacation introduction thing was going from one kid to another, up one aisle and down the next. Until it reached me and stopped dead.

I sprang to my feet and said, "Yes, Sister," though I had no idea why. I wanted to make sure she knew I agreed with her, no matter what she had been talking about. I paused, then said, "My name is James John Pa—"

"I know who *you* are, Master Murphy," Sister

Angelica said. The *you* felt like a poke in the chest with one of my #2 pencils. She opened the drawer of her desk and pulled out a red folder. The name MURPHY was written on the front in big, bold letters. A red folder with your name on it in big, bold letters is not a good sign, in case you hadn't guessed. "All your previous teachers have told me about you and your" — she held up the folder and waved it around a little, and then she stood even taller, if that was possible — "your various antics. I want you to know from the start that I will not tolerate any such behavior here. None. Am I clear, Master Murphy?"

"Yes, Sister." I did have questions, though. Like what exactly had these teachers said about me, and was it all really true? Even a murderer gets a trial with a lawyer who can ask questions and explain why his client did whatever he did. I knew that because my uncle Arthur was a lawyer. And did Sister Angelica really have to say all this so the whole class could hear? She could have called me aside at the end of class and . . .

". . . take your desk to the back of the room, Master Murphy."

"Huh?"

Her eyes were wide open, boring into me, and

not in a friendly way. "You need to pay better attention." This time that long, bony finger pointed over my shoulder toward the back of the room. "Take your desk there, next to Master Vero. Everyone else in the row should move their desks forward to fill in the empty space."

I picked up the desk and began making my way back toward Vero, who seemed both relieved that he wasn't Sister Angelica's target anymore and a little distressed at my fate. Some kids were laughing, of course. No surprise there. Everyone enjoys a show like this, especially when they aren't the star.

Then I spotted Kathy Gathers in the fourth row. She had her fingers over her mouth, trying unsuccessfully to hold in her giggling. I felt my face flush with embarrassment, and I looked away so quickly that my new pencil box slid off my desk and hit Roger Sutternhopf right in the head. The entire class erupted in a roar of laughter.

"He hit me in the head, Sister Angelica," Roger blurted out, grabbing his skull as if I'd hit him with a ball-peen hammer. This little act of Roger's only made everyone laugh harder. "He did it on purpose, too!"

"Boys and girls, please settle down." Sister Angelica clapped her hands. "And Master Murphy. Try to be more careful in the future."

I didn't even say "Yes, Sister." I was too humiliated and angry. I mean, I hadn't done anything at all, but I was being sent to the back of the room and being laughed at by all sixty-one of my classmates. Including Kathy Gathers.

There was lots of scraping noise as all the kids in my row scooted their desks forward while still sitting in them. I put my desk down next to Vero's and sank into it. Ellen McDonald appeared a second later with my bruised pencil box and put it on my desk, whispering, "I'm sorry, Jimmy," before hurrying back to her desk.

I might have mumbled "Thanks" to her, but I can't remember. A numb feeling was creeping up the back of my neck and invading my brain, completely blocking out everything else. I wasn't thinking anything in particular. It was like a giant electrical storm flashing and exploding in my brain.

Sister Angelica instructed us to take out our math books and open to page 14. I did as directed, but I wasn't thinking about math or page 14 or anything else except that I hated Sister Angelica Rose. With a passion.

I shoved my pencil box into the space under the desk. So much for new beginnings, I thought. From my right, Philip whispered, *"Hostis humani generis."*

2

The Plot Sickens

"I HATE HER for that." That wasn't me talking about what had happened to me, though I completely agreed. It was Vero who said it. He was a good pal, always ready to defend anyone who had a nun encounter like mine.

"Me, too," said Iggy. We were on the lunch line, sliding our green plastic trays along the aluminum railing and trying not to gag. The first item offered was always the brown soup, which smelled like it came directly from the boys' bathroom. Mom volunteered as a lunch aide when she wasn't working at my dad's office, and when I asked her what was in the brown soup, she said, "You don't want to know, Jimmy."

After the brown soup came hockey puck hamburgers with gooey yellow glop on top, hot dogs boiled to a strange gray-pink color, and a vat of chicken chow mein. When I asked Mom what was in the chow mein, she suggested that I have the brown soup instead.

I was about to grab a simple and safe American cheese sandwich on white bread when long metal barbecue tongs suddenly appeared in front of my face.

"Jimmy," a familiar voice said, "you should try one of these chicken cutlets. They're new on the menu."

My cousin Sophia was wagging the chicken cutlet up and down in a way that made it impossible for me to move forward without smacking into it. Actually, she wasn't my cousin. She was my mom's nephew's second cousin once removed, or something like that. I could never keep track of all the branches of the Italian side of the family tree, so everyone was an aunt, uncle, or cousin to me. "It looks good, don't you think?" she asked.

I liked Sophia. She laughed and smiled a lot when the family got together at holidays and funerals, and she told the best jokes, too. And when my family visited hers, she always gave me a little glass of red wine with dinner, whispering, "Don't tell I gave you this."

I stared at the cutlet, wondering what part of a chicken was so perfectly round. I was about to say no thanks, but Sophia was still beaming a one-hundred-watt smile and I didn't want to disappoint her. I said okay, and she put the cutlet on a plate, then ladled gravy over it.

"Thanks, Sophia," I said quietly, putting the plate on my tray. I grabbed a carton of milk and followed Jimmy Mayor as he headed for the table where we usually sat.

I wasn't watching where Mayor was going. I was staring at the gravy on my plate. It was a shiny, greasy light brown, slick with little ribbons of dark color in it that swirled and circled the cutlet. The dark part looked like worms trying to attack the chicken.

The idea of worms in my food made my stomach do a flip-flop, and I tasted a little bit of puke in my mouth. I thought I might hurl for real, so I looked away, and the first person I made eye contact with was Kathy Gathers, who was sitting at a table with six of her girlfriends. As soon as she spotted me, she started laughing, and so did her friends. One of them whispered something in her ear, and Kathy laughed even harder. Suddenly that plastic tray felt as heavy as my desk.

I turned away quickly so Kathy wouldn't see me blushing, but my eyes fastened on those ribbon worms. They were wriggling around like crazy now and seemed to be coming for me. That made my stomach do a double flip-flop. I closed my eyes and started to walk faster, but Mayor had stopped, so I rammed him in the back with my tray. And that got the ribbon worms really shaking around.

"Hey," Mayor said quietly to a little kid at our table. Mayor's hair was always a crewcut shaved down to the wood, which gave him a serious, down-to-business military look. "We have to have a meeting, so we need this table."

The kid looked startled, but didn't say no, so Mayor pressed on. "Murph here"—he nodded his fuzzy head in my direction—"had a bad morning, and we have to plan what to do, you know what I mean?" Mayor was one smooth operator. His dad owned five or six insurance offices in New Jersey, and Mayor was always visiting one or another of them and sitting in on meetings. He knew how to get things done without a lot of fuss.

"Ah, I guess," the kid said. But he didn't move. He had very big, very brown eyes that seemed slightly startled because a sixth grader was actually talking to him.

Mayor gave him a smile and asked, "What grade

are you in, um . . ." The "um" kind of hung in the air a long time.

"Alan," the kid finally replied. "Alan Craig. I'm in second grade."

"Hey, do you have a sister in fifth grade? Elaine, right? Blond hair? Pretty?"

"Yeah, I guess," said Alan the Second Grader, shrugging his shoulders a little.

"Good to meet you, Al. Hey, could you move down a few seats so Murph can sit on the aisle?" Then he said in a confidential whisper, "We have to settle some business, Al. Know what I mean?"

"Yeah." Al the Second Grader picked up his tray and moved down to the far end of the table. We filled in the rest of the seats, with me on the aisle, Mayor next to me, then Squints, and Al the Second Grader next to him. Vero, Iggy, Philip, and Tom-Tom were across from us.

"Okay. After what Angelica did to Murph and Philip, we need a plan to take care of her," Mayor began, "before it's too late."

"Philip?" I asked. Mayor didn't hesitate. Seems that while I was in my new beginning—Kathy Gathers daydream, Angelica had called on Philip to say his name and tell about his summer. He stood up like everyone else and said, *"Mi nombre es . . ."* She wouldn't let him finish. Instead, she said, "This year everything will be said in English, Philip, starting now."

Philip was as thin as a piece of dental floss and just as pale, and being forced to speak English must have been excruciating for him. His ears and cheeks were still burning a furious red.

"Who's Angelica?" Al the Second Grader asked. "And before what's too late?"

"Hey, shut up, kid." That was Squints, who never took a subtle approach when a direct attack was available. "I mean," he continued, peering around at all of us through the thick lenses of his glasses, "why are we talking to a second grader?"

Tom-Tom grunted in agreement. He was thin and tall—half a head taller than Iggy's hair—with a long, serious face. Tom-Tom's real name was Toma Capreanu Baiat (which means Thomas the Goat Boy in Romanian), and even though his family had been in Kearny for years, he still had a slight accent that made everything he said seem wise and important. Sort of like a very intelligent Count Dracula. "You should listen more," he told Al the Second Grader. "You will learn something that way."

"Angelica," Mayor told Al in a perfectly pleasant voice. Most kids in the older grades dropped the "Sister" part of a nun's name (unless, of course, the nun was nearby). Al was only in second grade, but by fourth grade he'd be doing it too. "She's new, and she gave both Murph and Philip a hard time this morning. And for no good reason, either." There was a low grumble of approval from my friends that made me feel less alone. "And we want to be sure it doesn't happen again." Another set of approving animal growls.

"Now," Mayor said, eyeing everyone at the table, "we need to know our goal, and we need a plan to achieve that goal." Spoken like a true insurance man.

"Goals shmoals," Squints muttered. "Let's just *do* something!"

Tom-Tom seconded Squints's demand with a solemn nod of his head, adding, "Yes, it is no time to waste time."

"We can't just *do* something unless we know what we're planning to *do*."

Mayor was working hard to keep everyone focused and under control. But I wasn't paying close attention. Glancing between Vero and Iggy, I could see the back of Kathy's head. She leaned a little to her right and said something to one of her friends.

That friend leaned toward the girl next to her and said something that was passed around their table to much laughter.

"Maybe we can torture her," Iggy suggested. "Put bugs in her desk. Hide all the chalk . . ."

"Yeah." Squints sounded as if he'd been given a present. "We could . . . we could . . ." Suddenly Squints was so enthusiastic, his words got stuck together the way Philip's did when he spoke in English. "We could lock the supply closet the next time she leaves the key and . . . and . . . and then throw the key away. We could . . . we could glue her desk drawers shut. We could . . . we could . . ."

Squints and everyone else at the table suddenly went dead quiet as Sister Regina stopped next to me. She was one of three nuns on aisle patrol today, strolling around to make sure everyone was behaving properly.

Sister R was okay in my book. She always spoke in a quiet whisper and had never hit anyone, as far as I knew. Which was not only unusual but an important personal characteristic to someone who seemed to be a natural nun target. Most of the nuns had a simple crucifix, two inches tall and black with a silver Christ hanging on it. But Sister R had the coolest, most gruesome crucifix dangling from her waist. It was four or five inches long and had painted blood dripping down Christ's hands and feet.

"Boys," she said in a soft, angelic voice, "we need to keep our voices down in the cafeteria, okay? And James, you should finish up your lunch. There are children starving in Armenia, you know."

I said I would, and she drifted down the aisle, scanning tables and chatting with kids.

Squints adjusted his oversize black-rimmed glasses and tried to get back into telling us what we could do to Angelica. But he'd lost momentum and could only sputter, "Um . . . um . . . we could . . . you know . . ."

"I'll tell you what we can do," Vero said in a hoarse whisper. He put his elbows on the table and leaned over his tray, then gave everyone a dark, no-nonsense glare. "We could annihilate her," he began. "We could decimate her, lacerate and mutilate her. We could eradicate and emasculate her—"

"Emasculate?" Iggy asked. "That's technically not possible." Iggy's real name was Richard French, but he got his nickname because he was always talking about the International Geophysical Year. Hundreds of scientists around the world were doing research on gravity, cosmic rays, and weather patterns, though he always lost me when he got to hard solar corpuscular radiation. In other words, he liked things to be scientifically accurate.

But Vero wasn't about to be stopped by scientific reality. He was on a roll. "W-we need to invalidate, detonate, terminate, and murderlate her to pieces."

"Murderlate?" was murmured by everyone at the table, including Al the Second Grader, with some confused looks tossed around besides.

After a second of silence, Squints demanded, "What does that mean?"

Vero looked shocked. Maybe because he just realized he'd made up a word and wasn't exactly sure how to explain it. Philip came to the rescue with *"Obit anus, abit onus."* He nodded his head in a dead serious way, as if that settled everything.

Squints would have none of it. "Jeez, Philip, can you translate for once?"

Philip seemed startled by the request, especially after what had happened to him in class that morning. But Squints was a friend and wasn't being mean like Sister Angelica. "It . . . it . . . it m-m-means . . . Th . . . th . . ."

"Spit it out already," Squints ordered. Which you don't ever want to say to Philip, because he will.

"Th . . . th . . . the old woman di-di-dies, th . . . the bu-bu-bu-burden is lifted."

Squints's face lit up. "Ah," he said in a hushed voice. "Killing Sister Angelica Rose. Has a nice sound to it."

Of course, we all knew he wasn't suggesting that we actually murder Angelica. Though I admit I had homicidal feelings about her. But getting even some-how, embarrassing her the way she embarrassed me and Philip, sounded good. A loud discussion imme-diately began on ways to murderlate-embarrass Sister Angelica. I didn't say a word, because I was trying to work out another, more immediate problem. Sister R had made it to the end of the cafeteria and was now slowly circling back our way. I had to get rid of my worm-squirming chicken cutlet or she would make me eat it, probably while she watched.

If I'd had some mashed potatoes or a bunch of string beans, I would have buried the cutlet under them and hoped that Sister R didn't notice. This strat-egy worked at home maybe sixty-two percent of the time, which is decent enough odds. A napkin would have worked too, but as usual I hadn't taken one and neither had any of the other guys. This is why we all went home every day with a greasy smudge near our right pants pocket (except for Mayor, who's left-handed, so his smudge is near his left pocket).

Sister R was closing in on our table, so I had to act fast. I gagged a little bit, but I managed to pick up the cutlet between my thumb and forefinger and hold it under the table. Now what was I supposed to do? Just then, Sister R's shadow fell across my tray, and the entire table went dead quiet again. "Are we all finished here, boys?" she asked in a sunny, soft voice. "Why don't you take your trays to the counter, then go outside to play."

After a unanimous "Yes, Sister," the guys all pushed their chairs back to stand up. Except me. I was trying to figure out how to get up, take hold of my tray, and not let her see . . .

This was the moment when the greasy cutlet, alive with predatory worms, slipped between my fingers and sailed to freedom. The next second, Sister R was looking down and wearing a completely baffled expression.

I leaned over the end of the table and looked down too. There, perched delicately on the very tip of one of Sister R's sensible black shoes, was my perfectly round chicken cutlet.

"Master Murphy," Sister R said with a tired sigh, "sometimes you would try the patience of a saint."

I was still studying the cutlet and wondering how it could possibly stick to such a gleaming piece of shiny leather. And here is where my brain decided to abandon and betray me. Which it did frequently. Instead of having me apologize and scramble to get the cutlet off her shoe, it made me remember the shoes Ellen McDonald wore last Easter.

Ellen's shoes were black patent leather and so shiny you could see your reflection in them. I know that because I was trying to position myself to find out if it was really true that you could see a girl's underwear by looking at her patent leather shoes. But what caught my eye instead were the tiny red bows right at the tips of Ellen's shoes. I suddenly pictured Sister R and all the other nuns wearing shoes with tiny red bows on them. And this started me chuckling.

Maybe I was nervous from the morning's encounter. Maybe I was nervous that Sister R might be ticked off enough to smack me in the head with her blood-dripped crucifix. When I looked up and saw Vero's face, his eyes had become dinner plates in panic, so naturally I burst out laughing. And not quietly, either.

"Urphy-may," Vero hissed under his breath in his best pig Latin, "ix-nay on the aff-lay." He was vigorously nodding his head toward Sister R.

Vero was looking so serious that his warning set me off laughing even harder, and this got Tom-Tom, Squints, and Philip laughing too. By this time, kids from surrounding tables were watching us, some standing up to get a better view. Even Kathy Gathers had turned around. It's amazing how a little chicken cutlet can attract a crowd.

"I think," Sister R said as softly as ever, but with a tiny edge to each word, "you should go to the principal's office and explain to Sister Rose Mary what happened here. The rest of you boys should settle down now, or you'll be joining him."

I picked up my tray, walked quickly around Sister R, and headed down the aisle. I didn't even check to see if Kathy Gathers was watching my latest humiliation. All I heard was Sister R asking for something to take the chicken cutlet off her shoe and then saying, "None of you boys has a napkin? How is that possible . . . ?"

3

A Rose by Any Other Name

I GAVE MY TRAY to one of the lunch ladies (who was really Mary Claire Danes's mom). Sophia waved her barbecue tongs at me and asked if I liked the chicken. I said it had been an interesting experience. Then I headed for the exit.

Sister Rose Vincent was standing guard at the door to head off any escapees. When I was little, I thought all nuns were seven feet tall. I was taller now and knew they really weren't, but Sister Rose Vincent was way over six feet tall and very big in every direction. She looked like a giant black billowing mountain with a tiny carved pinhead stuck on top.

In all my years at St. Stephen's, Sister Rose Vincent had never, ever smiled or said very much to me. A "don't do that" here or a "can you please be quiet" there, but mostly she just frowned when she saw me. I was sure she had some really good stuff to add to the red MURPHY folder. As I got nearer the door, her eyes were drilling into me, so I told her, "I'm supposed to go to Sister Rose Mary's."

"Hrrrumph." I thought that was nun-speak for *I would expect nothing less from a troublemaker like you.* I pushed the door open, and she added, "And don't dawdle in the halls."

The last thing anyone wanted to do was dawdle in the halls of St. Stephen's. Every time the last person left a classroom, the lights were turned off to save money. When the last class left a hallway or wing of the building, those lights were turned off too. It wasn't just the spooky darkness that kept us from goofing around in the hallways. The nuns and their black robes blended into the darkness, as if they could will themselves to be a part of the shadows, ever ready to strike. Like a green snake in the grass, only deadlier.

I took the dark, gloomy stairs two at a time and was on the main floor in a few seconds. A couple of weak overhead lights were left on in the main hall leading to the principal's office, probably so parents coming to pick up sick kids wouldn't get lost in the dark. A thin finger of light let me see the statue of Saint Stephen that was built into the wall next to

Sister Rose Mary's office, a saintly smile on his lips (which were painted a weird red) and a large stone in his right hand.

The story goes that long ago an angry mob stoned him to death because he was Catholic. Which does not sound like a fun way to go, if you ask me. But there he was anyway, smiling happily, as if to say *Hey, kid. Play your cards right and you too can wear lipstick and be pulverized to death.*

I crossed myself quickly for good luck as I walked past the statue and into the principal's outer office. I was about to say hello to Mrs. Branfurs, the school secretary (who was really Billy Branfurs's mom), when Sister Rose Mary came bustling out of her office. She had a wad of papers in one hand and the brass bell she rang to get the attention of noisy kids in the other. She glanced up from the papers, spotted me, and said, "Ah, we meet again, Master Murphy."

"Sister Regina sent me up to—"

"You can tell me your story later. I have to speak with Mrs. Durkin and Sister Dominick now and do some other chores around school." Sister Rose Mary was all of four feet six inches tall (if that), so I was taller than her by over a foot. Still, nobody ever messed with her.

She gave the papers to Mrs. Branfurs, along with some instructions. Sister Rose Mary was carrying the bell by the clapper so it wouldn't always be ringing. Her entire hand and part of her wrist were hidden inside it. The handle was sort of like a pirate's hook, only straight and pointy. She tapped me on the wrist with her pirate hand and added, "Stand there and watch the clock for fifteen minutes while I'm away. And don't fidget."

"Yes, Sister."

As she left the office, she added, "And think about your sins."

"Yes, Sister."

I had done clock-watch time before. Lots. So I took my place in the center of the room and stared at the clock. Mrs. Branfurs shuffled the papers, then began typing.

I took a deep breath and tried to relax. Watching a clock for fifteen minutes is a form of slow torture and must be against some United Nations war convention rules. The clock ticks along, and you (meaning me) get to see the second hand click, click, click its slow way around the clock face, one tiny space at a time.

From experience, I knew that the best way to

get through this was to think about something else. Something that would take my brain on a little journey.

This is when I began thinking about roses. Not the flower kind, though my mom loved to grow them. I began thinking about the nun kind of Rose and how many of them we had at St. Stephen's. So many I could hardly keep them straight in my head.

To start, there was the principal, Sister Rose Mary. And Sister Angelica Rose, of course. And Sister Rose Vincent, no forgetting her. My brother, Jerry, was in eighth grade, and his teacher was named Sister Rose Edwards. And there was Sister Rose Ascenza, who was visiting from Italy, and Sister Rose of Lima, who was here from Peru. Oh, and there was Sister Immaculata Rose.

Most nuns seemed old to me, but Sister Immaculata was really old, and by old I mean ancient. She could have been there to help push the stone from Jesus's grave on Easter morning. She didn't teach anymore, just hung around the convent, which was right behind the school. Once a day she took a stroll up Beech Street, the dead-end side street where the school and convent were. "Taking a stroll" suggests that she had some speed in her step, but she actually doddered along at about ten feet an hour, saying her rosary. Everybody on the street knew and liked Sister Immaculata, and some people put benches on their front lawns near the sidewalk so she could stop and rest along the way.

I came out of my Rose nun thoughts to discover that only four minutes and twenty-two seconds had clicked by. Darn. Not fair, I thought. Here, of course, my brain took charge, and I heard myself thinking that what really wasn't fair was the way Sister Angelica had singled me out, which made Kathy Gathers laugh at me, and that I was doing clock-watch time. Though I admit that laughing when I saw the chicken cutlet on Sister R's shoe wasn't very smart.

Still, it wasn't fair. I'd come to school hoping to change, but they wouldn't let me. Sister Angelica wouldn't let me! I remembered the way she looked at me — like I was a predatory worm — and I found my brain going dark and darker until I was sure it was twisting itself into a brain knot. Then I remembered Kathy Gathers laughing at me, and my heart started racing with anger.

I looked at the clock. Still six long minutes to go. Tick. Tick. Tick. Tick. The second hand moved along very, very, *very* slowly. The back of my head seemed to be going numb as I watched the second hand. Tick. Tick. Tick. Tick. I got angrier and angrier with every tick of the clock. This. Tick. Is. Tick. Not. Tick. Fair. Tick. This is not fair. This is not fair . . .

In some far-off part of the school, Sister Rose Mary began ringing her bell. I closed my eyes tight, then opened them. I could see through the office windows that clouds had blocked out the light. Or was that gloomy darkness just in my head? No, there were ominous-looking clouds moving in. Way off to the left, there was a really dark patch of sky that looked like a purple-green bruise. It was going to rain, and hard. I hoped I could get home before the storm.

I shook my head to refocus my wandering thoughts. Or, as Mayor might suggest, to make a plan. Step one was simple. I needed to figure out how to murderlate-embarrass Sister Angelica. In a big, gigantic way that fit my rage. The guys were working on that while I was watching the second hand, so I didn't have to worry about it just now. Step two would be harder. I needed to figure out how to win over Kathy Gathers.

I reminded myself that it was only the first day of school, so I could still show her that I wanted to change. Yes, she'd laughed at me. Twice. But I'd been laughed at since kindergarten, so that was nothing new. Exactly how to impress her escaped my brain, but I knew I could figure it out . . .

"Ah, James," Mrs. Branfurs said in a whisper, "you might want to stand up straight. Sister Rose Mary will be on her way back."

I snapped to attention and took a deep breath. I could almost feel Sister Rose Mary's pirate hand poking me in the ribs as she lectured me about wasting food, kids starving in Armenia, and laughing inappropriately.

"I wouldn't worry," Mrs. Branfurs added, her voice even softer. "She has a meeting with a parent in" — she looked at her watch — "five minutes and won't have much time."

Even though I was still standing as straight as an iron pole, I felt myself relax inside. "Thanks," I whispered. Some adults know exactly what to say and are even nice enough to say it.

Sister Rose Mary ghosted back into her office, looked at me as if she didn't know why I was there, then told me she had spoken to Sister Regina and that I could go to my class. Like most nuns, she added something as I made my escape. "And let's not let this happen again."

I kind of drifted through the rest of the afternoon. I caught up with my class just as they were going back inside, so I didn't hear anything about the Plan. When Sister Angelica had her back to us, writing something or other on the blackboard, Vero leaned over to let me know what they had talked about. He was whispering so softly I could barely hear a word. Even so, that whisper didn't get past Sister Angelica.

"Master Vero," she said, not even bothering to turn around, "your friend doesn't need any further distractions or trouble today."

Vero and I looked at each other. She hadn't taken her eyes off the blackboard, so how did she know what was going on behind her?

"Um, yes, Sister." Vero sat up in his desk, a puzzled look on his face. I think nuns have weird alien powers. There's simply no other way to explain it.

4

The Almost Plan

IT WAS BEGINNING to rain when school got out. Just a sprinkle, but that really nasty-looking section of sky was right overhead and there were some rumbles of thunder. You could tell it was going to let loose any second. The guys and I split up and headed for home, moving fast.

I was in such a hurry that I didn't stop to get my usual bag of salty potato sticks at the store across from school. And I hardly thought about the three high school girls I usually passed on the way home. I didn't know them, but I had noticed them for the first time in fifth grade, around when I started really liking Kathy Gathers. They always wore short plaid skirts in different colors and matching tight sweaters, and they said "Hello, handsome" to me whenever we passed on the sidewalk. Which made me blush. In a way that felt good.

I did stop briefly on the bridge over the train tracks to pick up a penny. My mom said it was bad luck to leave an orphaned penny on the ground, and I didn't need any more bad luck that day. Not with Sister Angelica gunning for me.

Rain started falling hard when I was still a block from home, so I was drenched when I finally pushed open our front door.

My mom worked as my dad's receptionist-book-keeper most days, and Jerry was out, probably off at his friend's house down the block, playing penny ante poker. So I was alone in the house. Which was fine. I liked being by myself. Only with the day I had had, plus the rain and my soggy clothes, a cloud of gloom kept following me from room to room. Not even watching cartoons on television was enough to distract me.

I wondered what the guys had said about mur-derlating Sister Angelica. As we were leaving school, Mayor said they had some ideas, but he didn't have time to give me any details. Except that Al the Second Grader was definitely a deranged individual in a helpful sort of way. Which meant that all I could do at the moment was figure out how to change Kathy Gathers's opinion of me.

I could try to actually study harder to improve my pitiful grades. I'd always brought some books home, mostly so Mom wouldn't ask why I hadn't brought any books home. Unfortunately, I was so angry at Angelica that I hadn't copied the day's assignments from the blackboard, so I had no idea what I was supposed to read or do.

Philip's house was right behind mine. I could go to his window and ask him for the assignments. And find out if he knew anything more about the emerging Plan. His bedroom was on the side of his house next to our back property line, and sometimes we talked (as much as Philip ever talked, that is) back there. But the rain was coming down in buckets, and going to his house seemed like a lot of work. I could call him, but he'd probably think it was weird if I suddenly started asking about homework on the phone. No sixth-grade guy ever did that.

I decided that the only thing I could do was pay better attention tomorrow. Tomorrow would be plenty soon to start studying.

But I needed to do something right away to show

Kathy that I'd changed. Or at least wanted to change. *Write another story* popped into my head. No, no, no. Even if I wrote a great Kathy Gathers story where she was thin and gorgeous and nuclear-scientist smart (and she's all of those in real life), she'd be suspicious. And I had promised not to write any more stories about her, and I never, ever break a promise. So what could I do?

The mind works in mysterious ways. At least mine does. For some reason I thought about the star-shaped scar on my right arm where Sister Anita had stabbed me with her yellow ballpoint pen just before last Easter. She tried to say it had been an accident, but I don't think anyone in the class believed that. Anyway, for some completely weird reason I thought about putting a tattoo there. Of Kathy's initials.

It was a brilliant idea. So brilliant I started to smile.

Naturally, I couldn't get a real tattoo. But I'd drawn tattoos on my arm in the past (mostly the uniform numbers of baseball players I liked), so I knew that a black ballpoint pen would be a decent substitute. And I could darken it whenever it started to fade.

I went upstairs three steps at a time, tossed my wet shirt onto the bathroom floor, and toweled my right arm dry. There was my scar, about one inch across. A few days after the stabbing, the puncture wound had become infected and ugly, and when the scab finally fell off a few weeks later, voilà, there was a scar, looking like an exploding red star.

I found a pen in my room, then went back to the bathroom, where I stood sideways in front of the mirror. Now, doing an ink tattoo left-handed while looking into a mirror isn't easy. Try it and you'll understand why. Everything is backwards and turned around. My eyes kind of crossed when I tried to position the pen point, and even concentrating real hard, I began writing the letter *K* backwards. Not a good start. Which seemed to be the theme of my whole day.

I was able to calm myself when I realized it was only a small line and not a major flub. I went back to work and did a really good job. The star scar was right between the two letters, **K ★ G**, high enough up on my arm to be covered by a short-sleeved shirt. I could keep my tattoo hidden from my parents and snoopy teachers but let Kathy see it when I wanted to.

I checked it in the mirror and even flexed my muscles to see if it rippled the way tattoos do in the movies. I suddenly had another brilliant idea. I found a pen with red ink and began coloring in the star to deepen the red. The finished project looked downright artistic, if I say so myself.

I studied my new tattoo a couple of times from different perspectives. Okay, I studied it seven or eight times and even used a handheld mirror to check it out up close. This close-up look started me wondering if the red scar thing might look a little too much like blood, and some people (Kathy?) might think it was weird. After a moment of panic (I get these from time to time), I put on a T-shirt that covered the tattoo. I could scrub the red star extra hard over the next week and slowly tone down the color. Until then, I would keep my work of art hidden.

An hour later my brother came home, said "Hey," and punched me hard in the tattooed arm. "How'd your day go?" he asked.

"The pits."

"Good old St. Stephen's," he said. He stuck his head into the refrigerator, searching for something to eat. "You should have seen Rose Edwards in action today." He emerged from the refrigerator with an orange and began to peel it. "Rick was messing around, making all sorts of mouth noises, and she winged a big pink eraser at him. He was, like, fifty feet away, but she nailed him square in the nose. She's got some arm."

"Cool," I said. Lots of nuns tossed stuff at kids, but most weren't very accurate. It was good to know which ones were and be ready to duck.

My mom came home next and started making dinner.

"How was your day, Jimmy?"

"Okay."

"Anything interesting happen?"

"Not really."

She looked up from cutting a carrot and seemed genuinely sad. "Don't worry. You'll have plenty of adventures this year."

"I can't wait," I mumbled.

Dad was visiting a client in Hoboken, so he got home last. He kissed Mom hello, then sat in his big armchair next to the fireplace in the living room, crossed his legs, and started to read the *Newark Star-Ledger*. After a few minutes he called out to Mom in the kitchen.

"Did you see this article, Helen? That bridge they put up two years ago is already falling apart. Shoddy materials."

"Doesn't surprise me. All politicians are crooks."

It had really been a terrifically crappy first day of school, and even that little recollection got my brain buzzing again like a pissed-off bee. To calm it, I remembered the punch hello from my brother, encouragement from Mom, Dad reading the paper and chatting with Mom about the news. These things meant that all was right with the world just now. Except, of course, for Sister Angelica Rose, who was probably back there in the convent inventing new ways to torture me. At least there would be a long night before my next humiliation.

5

My Cherry Jell-O Backbone

HERE'S THE PROBLEM with going to sleep. You close your eyes, all relaxed, and a second later it's morning and you have to go back to school. Back to the big brick torture chamber. All I could do was hope for a better day and maintain a low profile. As in, will myself to become invisible.

School started out fine. In the big playground before the bell rang, Mayor and Iggy gave me the update on murderlating Angelica. Lots of ideas had been tossed around, I was told, but Al the Second Grader came up with the most imaginative one. He wanted to dig a big hole where Sister Angelica would walk, stud the bottom with long, sharp, pointy punji sticks, and then hide the hole with grass. Angelica comes strolling along, completely unaware of the trap, and then *pow*, she falls in and is skewered like a wienie on a stick.

This would be a little more severe than embarrassing her, but I liked the image of a stuck Sister Angelica. Then I saw a problem. "Ah, Mayor—"

"Yeah, yeah, we know," Mayor said, clearly frustrated.

The catch was obvious. The outside spaces around St. Stephen's and the convent were either concrete or asphalt. Or iron grates where water drained off. Inside the school grounds there was one tiny patch of dirt with two spindly pine trees and a couple of other miserable-looking plants, but it was to the side of the asphalt, up against the building, and nobody actually walked there.

"But don't worry, Murph. We haven't given up. And Al said he'd study his G.I. Joe and horror comics for more ideas." True to his professional calling, Mayor decided we'd have another meeting at lunchtime. "And why the long-sleeved shirt? It's gonna be hot today."

I grabbed the area where my tattoo was to make sure it was truly hidden. "Ah, all my other shirts were dirty."

In class I decided to lie low. Literally. I slid down in my chair until my back and head were nearly parallel with the floor. This way I could avoid being spotted and having to answer any of those questions teachers always seem to be coming up with. It took Sister Angelica all of one minute and twenty-eight seconds to scope me out and say, "Master Murphy. Is your backbone made of cherry Jell-O today?"

This comment, of course, made everyone sitting in front of me — which meant the whole class, including you-know-who — turn to see what I was up to. Oh, yeah, and laugh. I touched my arm where the tattoo was, this time for moral support.

I was also kind of flustered, and my brain seemed to go into a fast spin cycle. I came within an inch of saying *I like orange Jell-O better,* in an attempt to make an awkward situation funny. But I managed to hold it in as I struggled to get myself into a sitting position. Naturally my knees came up hard and jammed tight under the desktop, and I would have tipped over if Vero hadn't caught me and my desk before I hit the floor.

"Class, class," Angelica called, shaking her head. She clapped her hands several times to get everyone's attention. "Please, let's not give the class clown an audience. Eyes forward, everyone." As everyone was turning back to face her, she gave me a frosty look that would have iced a chrome car bumper until it shattered.

After this, I came up with another way to remain unseen. When Angelica walked to the right side of the room, I leaned slightly to the left—enough to be behind Joey Spano and out of her sight. When she went to the left, I leaned right. Back and forth, back and forth for the rest of the morning. It was exhausting work. Luckily, Joey is a pretty big kid and hard to see through, so I was able to get into a kind of rhythm.

The lunchtime meeting didn't produce any new ideas, although Al the Second Grader was very enthusiastic about attempting to electrocute Angelica or arranging an accidental tumble down a flight of stairs. I thought these possibilities might be worth considering, but Mayor explained that we weren't trying to injure or kill Sister Angelica. Al the Second Grader didn't seem to hear. In fact, his eyes went all deep and scary-mysterious, as if he were thinking over a hundred painful ways to deal with Sister Angelica, and I really started to like the kid. On the plus side, Sister Regina stopped by our table while patrolling and was very happy to see that I was eating a simple, non-grease-slicked American cheese sandwich. "But

James," she whispered, leaning so close her crucifix clinked against the table, "maybe we should keep our hands above the table." She glanced quickly down at her shoes, then smiled. "Just to be on the safe side."

By two o'clock in the afternoon I was feeling confident that I might escape the day with only the cherry Jell-O incident added to my red folder. This got me wondering what had made her say cherry Jell-O instead of just Jell-O. Maybe she really liked cherry Jell-O and was thinking about it and hoping they had it for dinner in the convent that night. And this notion got me wondering what nuns really ate over there, or if they ate anything except our immortal souls.

Next I remembered — don't ask, I don't know why; it's my brain's fault — the night last summer when Mom served orange Jell-O with canned pineapple chunks in it for dessert. Dad took a scornful look at it and said, "Those are pineapple, right?" "Yes," Mom answered. "You know I don't like pineapple," my dad stated, as if it had been written into the United States Constitution so we should all know it. "In any form."

"I don't neither," I said.

"Either," Mom corrected me. My brother snickered, and I felt as if everyone in class were looking at me again.

"Either or neither, I don't like the stuff."

"You will have a 'no thank you' portion," Mom told me firmly. She gave Dad a look that said *See what you've done?*—a look I'd gotten from nuns many times over the years.

It really wasn't fair that Mom got to pull out the "'no thank you portion'" line when I didn't have any lines to pull out on any occasion . . .

Suddenly Sister Angelica's voice broke into my thoughts: "Everyone, please take out your pencil and a piece of lined paper. In the time remaining before dismissal, we'll have a pop quiz on last night's history assignment."

There were groans and grumbles from just about everyone. Even the good-smart kids. And a few cusses from the other guys in the back row. A pop quiz was simply unfair on the second day of school. I didn't mumble a sound. I hadn't read anything at all the night before, and I just knew I was cooked.

As directed, I wrote my name and the date on the top line. For some reason, I always dated my papers April 1, but I usually put down the correct year. I also put JMJ in bold letters at the top of the paper, hoping that having Jesus, Mary, and Joseph hovering up there would give me good luck. Probably wouldn't, especially if you (meaning me) didn't study, but it couldn't hurt, right? You never know who might be gazing down upon you and feeling generous.

There were twenty questions on the quiz. Some true or false, most multiple-choice. Or in my case, multiple-guess. Sister Angelica said each question out loud, then wrote it down on the blackboard. She also said the possible multiple-choice answers and wrote them down too.

When the quiz was over, we passed our papers to the front, and she handed them out so that we could grade other kids' answers. It was, as Vero whispered, an inspired way for her to avoid doing work.

I knew perfectly well that I wouldn't get a very good grade. There was nothing new in that. But then she had the kids stand up and say the name of the person whose paper they had marked and the grade, which she wrote down in a book. More grumbles from the back row, since we knew what that would mean.

And so it began. Erin (Margaret) O'Connor was first to stand and read the score. "Roger Vandercleef Sutternhopf," she said loudly. "Ninety-five percent."

There were some "oohs" and "ahhs" at the near-perfect grade, and Roger looked around with a big grin on his face. I wasn't thinking about Roger or his grade. I was thinking that Roger sat in the seventh row, just to my left, so maybe they wouldn't get to my row for a while. And with sixty-two papers to go through, maybe the bell would ring to end the day, and I could escape. But which row had gotten my row's papers?

Turned out to be the eighth and last row, over by the windows. The third person in that row, Carol Brent, stood and said, "James Murphy." In a near whisper she quickly added, "Um, thirty."

There were more "oohs" and "ahhs," but they didn't sound like the ones Roger got. Most times I scored a little better than that because I usually made a decent number of lucky guesses.

"Master Murphy." Sister Angelica looked amazingly distressed and really unhappy, as if I'd run over a puppy with my bike. I mean, she seemed to take my grade as a direct insult aimed at her. "Did you read the assignment?"

I stood up slowly, trying to think of the best way to answer. I was kinda on trial here, since everyone in class was waiting to hear what I had to say, but I only noticed Kathy Gathers watching me. So I had to make this good. "Ah," I began. To say I had read the assignment would be to admit that I was too stupid to remember any of it. My brain tumbled around some ideas for an excuse, but panic set in and made all rational thought impossible. I finally decided I didn't have enough time to work out all the details. Instead, I said, "I meant to, Sister. Really, but . . . but . . . um . . .".

"Yes, I know," she said, cutting me off with a disgusted shake of her head. "And the road to hell is paved with good intentions." She shook her head again, her lips pursed as if she'd just sucked in the juice of twenty lemons. "Did you write down the assignments as I suggested yesterday?"

"Um . . ."

"And when you realized you hadn't" — now she was really heating up — "did you call one of your" — and here her face twisted in this dismissive way — "friends to see what the assignment was?"

"Well, um . . . no."

Sister Angelica's face had turned an intense shade of purple-red. Which is not good to add on top of annoyed, distressed, and disgusted. "Is there anyone you could call in the future to be sure you know what is expected?"

"Well, I guess . . ." I didn't offer any names, and

none of my friends chimed in to volunteer. As I said before, sixth-grade guys just didn't call each other to chat about homework.

There was another one of those embarrassingly long, deep silences. I wasn't sure what to say, so I didn't say anything. Sister Angelica looked troubled but wasn't offering a solution. Then a hand popped up a few seats in front of me.

"Sister?" a voice said.

Angelica located the raised hand. "Yes, Ellen?"

Ellen McDonald stood up. "He can call me to make sure he knows what the assignments are."

There were a few more "oohs," though these were different from the ones that came before because they were accompanied by some kissing sounds. Philip tossed in an "ooo-la-la" that didn't need translation.

I could feel my face flush. I wanted to yell out that I didn't want or need Ellen's help. But my brain started to explain to me that I *did* need help remembering assignments, but wouldn't it have been great if Kathy Gathers had been the one to volunteer.

"That's a very generous offer, Ellen. Very." The second "very" suggested that Sister Angelica would never, ever in her life have made such a kind offer herself for someone like me. "Master Murphy. You will get Ellen's phone number before you go home today, and be sure to call her tonight. At seven p.m. No more excuses for missed assignments. Am I clear?"

"Yes, Sister," I said, sliding back down into my seat. "Very."

6

Ken Gables Is Calling

BY THE TIME I got home, I was sweating bullets in my long-sleeved shirt. I went to change into a T-shirt and discovered that most of them had shrunk, maybe because I'd grown a few inches this year, and didn't completely hide the tattoo. I had to hunt hard to find a short-sleeved shirt that barely covered it. If only Sister Anita had stabbed me higher up the arm.

Got downstairs just as Jerry came home to punch me hello. Mom came charging in a little later, ordered me to set the table, and started making meatballs and spaghetti sauce. I got forks and knives, plates, and napkins and began setting them out on the dining room table.

In our old house we ate in the kitchen most nights. But when we moved to this house, we started eating in the dining room. Not because we turned fancy or anything. Because of the big red Nazi swastika on the kitchen floor.

When we came to look at this house for the first time, there was a round wooden table in the kitchen with a nice rug underneath. The day we moved in, the table and rug were gone, and there it was — a red swastika made of square floor tiles. The swastika must have been six feet across.

Both Mom and Dad began sputtering when they saw it, making these embarrassing "but . . . but . . . but" gasping sounds.

"That's weird," Jerry said.

"Bizarro," I added. "I have to tell Philip. He knows a lot about World War Two and stuff."

"Don't say a word to him. Or anybody else! They might think we put it there!" Dad barked. "Helen, go call Mr. Farina while I get something to cover this . . . this . . ." He pointed at it as if it were an extra-large bowl of orange Jell-O with pineapple chunks in it.

Mr. Farina was the real estate agent who had sold us the house. When he saw the swastika, he sputtered the way my parents had. And apologized, too. At first he tried to suggest that it might be some sort of symbol used by western Indians, but when my mom gave him "the look," he dropped that line of reasoning. "They seemed like such a nice couple," he said, referring to the elderly husband and wife who sold us the house. "Who would have guessed."

I had to agree. The husband and wife were both short and very round, like cream-filled doughnuts. At one point while we were looking at the house, the wife had said with great fondness, "We've had such nice times here. During the war we had our club meetings right here in the kitchen." Later I thought someone should have asked them what sort of club they hosted. I mean, Nazis in New Jersey! Who the heck knew?

Mr. Farina said he'd get the red tiles replaced with green ones that matched the rest of the floor. But the new tiles that arrived were a lot lighter than the old ones, and my parents decided that a fresh, minty green swastika was as bad as a blood-red one. So we still had the swastika, and now it looked as if the whole floor would have to be replaced to get rid of it. Until then, Dad refused to eat in the kitchen, period. He wouldn't even drink his evening bottle of Pepsi-Cola in there.

Table setting was an oddly important procedure in our house. Once, I complained to my mom about the silly, complicated rules for where the forks, knives, spoons, glasses, etc., etc., had to be put. Who decided this? I wanted to know. And why? And why did we have to follow those rules anyway? It wasn't as if the president would be coming for Mom's meatball and spaghetti dinner.

Mom looked perplexed about my rebellious attitude, then quoted some expert on the subject who obviously loved the idea of utensil and glassware rules. "A properly set table," Mom said in a serious voice, "is the canvas for a beautiful meal."

My mom's an artist. She cut out a piece of paper the same size as our place mats and drew in where everything was supposed to go, including which direction knife blades should face (toward the plate, in case you're wondering) and the position of the water glasses.

I had memorized the paper plan and could put everything on the table automatically. I was halfway through the chore when my brother suddenly asked, "So who's K.G.?"

K.G.? What was he . . . Then I remembered my tattoo. "Ah, nobody."

"Does my little brother have a girlfriend?"

"No, no." I glanced down where the tattoo was

and saw that my sleeve had ridden up. In a panic, I swiped it down to cover the black and red marks. "It's nothing. It's a baseball player's initials." My mind did a freaky fast search of baseball player names and came up with, "It's Ken Gables. He was a pitcher." This was one hundred percent true, but I couldn't remember who he played for or if he was any good.

"Yeah, right," Jerry said. "So why the red heart?"

Red heart? I picked up the sleeve and realized that in trying to wash off the red, I had dragged some of the ink down, so it did kinda look like a heart. A blurry one, but definitely a heart. I covered the tattoo up again.

"And not just a red heart," my brother added, "but a red 'I love you' heart."

"Shut up," I hissed. Panic was closely followed by brain sizzle and made any other reply impossible. I just stared at him and tried to gulp in air.

"So who exactly is this K.G.?"

"I told you already . . ."

Just then the phone in the kitchen rang, interrupting Jerry's interrogation. I thought I'd never heard a more welcome sound. Saved by the bell, I thought. Or whatever sound the phone made. Mom was rolling meatballs and asked Jerry to answer the phone. Jerry gave me a look that said *Yeah, right,* and left the dining room. I started tossing forks, knives, and spoons onto the table, thinking I'd finish up fast and flee to my room to hide until dinner was ready.

Of course I should have known better, considering the way my luck had been running lately. I was putting down the last spoons when my brother called from the kitchen. "Oh, Jim-mee," he said in this drawn-out, singsongy, annoying voice. "It's for you-ooo." There was a pause. "It's a girl."

I hustled into the kitchen to get the phone from him before he did any more damage. Mom said, "A girl?" in a somewhat concerned tone. Maybe she was worried that I'd taken up story writing again.

"It's okay, Mom," I said. "It's about homework."

I grabbed the phone from Jerry, grunted angrily at him, and put my hand over the receiver. As my brother strolled past, he whispered, "Ken Gables my ass."

When Jerry was out of the room, I grumbled and said "Yeah" into the receiver a little more sternly than I'd wanted. "I mean, hello."

"You were supposed to call at seven," Ellen said crisply. "You told Sister Angelica you would."

"I forgot," I said, which was true enough. "I was setting the table for dinner," I added lamely.

"You need to remember to call. And if you have to do something else first, you should call and let me know."

I didn't say anything.

"Okay?"

"Sure." I took the phone to the stairs leading to the basement and sat down. I had no idea why Ellen wanted to help me, of all people, but it was clear this was going to be just one of many long calls.

"So," Ellen began, "do you know what we're supposed to do for spelling?"

Now I had her! I had actually jotted down the spelling assignment, and even got Philip to fill me in on what else we had to do for homework. I figured that if I could show Ellen I had the assignments under control, she'd go away and not bother me anymore. "Yeah, take the ten words on the list and put them in a sentence. I wrote that down."

"Good. But you have to spell them correctly and you have to punctuate correctly, too. Have you done them yet?"

"I will. Don't worry."

"And for math . . ."

"I know what to do," I said confidently. And I told her what it was.

Only it wasn't. Angelica had assigned fifteen specific problems from the text, but Philip had copied some of the numbers down wrong. Even if I got the answers right, I'd still fail. As Ellen told me the correct problems to do, I realized I should probably tell Philip. This might violate the rule about sixth-grade guys talking about homework, but it seemed only fair.

The rest of the conversation went pretty much the same way, and I had a sinking feeling I wouldn't be getting rid of Ellen and her phone calls anytime soon. We ended with her saying we'd meet before school so she could go over my homework. Trust me, I tried to tell her this wasn't necessary, but Ellen could be very . . . I'm not sure how to put this . . . she could be very persistent.

Now I was trapped, and it was all Sister Angelica's fault. I knew I had to do better in school to win over Kathy Gathers, but this wasn't how I wanted to do it.

Dinner dragged along with the usual sort of chatter. "How was your day?" "Okay." "Did anything interesting happen?" "No."

The highlight of dinner came when there was a pause in this scintillating conversation and Jerry said,

"Jimmy was telling me all about this amazing Ken Gables superstar guy, right?" He looked at me and gave me an evil smile. I could tell he wasn't going to let me off the hook anytime soon. "Maybe he can tell us more about K.G."

7

Where Is Your Brain, Jimmy?

THE NEXT MORNING, I tried to slip into the big playground unnoticed and mingle in the crowd of screaming, running kids, hoping to avoid Ellen until the bell rang. No such luck. There she was, standing next to the metal playground gate, clutching her books to her chest, waiting, watching. I wondered if Sister Rose Vincent had given her guard duty instructions.

"You're late," she announced.

"My mom made bacon this morning," I said. I didn't know why that had anything to do with being late. I think talking with Ellen made me a little nervous.

"We don't have a lot of time, Jimmy. Let me see your math homework."

"I did all the problems," I announced proudly. I waved the paper in the air so she could see that I'd actually done an entire page of math and didn't really need her help to check it. But she snatched the paper out of my hand and started studying it as if she were searching for fingerprints at a crime scene. Every so often she shook her head a little, grimaced, then circled something with her pencil, using her books as a desk.

She handed the paper back to me. "You made some addition and subtraction mistakes on five of them. The ones I circled. The three multiple-choice questions are wrong, so you need to think those over."

I tried to weasel her into giving me the right answers, but she just said, "I'm supposed to *help* you find the answers, not give them to you." When I didn't say anything, she added in a nicer voice, "Just do your work carefully and you'll be okay. Did you do the spelling words?"

Again, I pulled out my homework, proud that I'd actually done it and secretly hoping this would convince her to leave me alone. She took the paper, looked at it, seemed startled. "There are supposed to be ten sentences."

"The assignment said 'put the words in a sentence.' See, I even copied the instructions down word for word from the board. And I put them all in a sentence and underlined them. It didn't say anything about ten sentences."

"The *implication* of the assignment was that each word gets its own sentence. Where is your brain, Jimmy?" She explained "implication" in several different ways that even a squirrel would understand. Then she took a deep breath and read my sentence out loud. "The <u>agony</u> of the western <u>states</u> in the nineteenth <u>century</u> was that the Indian <u>chiefs</u> didn't want to <u>labor</u> for peace or even <u>consider</u> living in <u>cottages</u>" — she gave me a look, then went on — "because they wanted to exist happily in <u>nature</u> with <u>raccoons</u>" — she stopped reading again and muttered something under her breath — "<u>raccoons</u> and other <u>mammals</u>."

Listening to her read my work had me beaming with pride. It was a very nice-sounding sentence, one I could be proud of. It had every word on the list in it, they were neatly underlined, and I know I spelled them all correctly.

"But . . . but . . . but . . ." She jabbed her finger at my sentence. "Cottages! What do Indians have to do with cottages? And raccoons! This is the silliest thing I've ever read."

I was really, really irked. My sentence did everything the assignment asked for, so why was Ellen so upset? And for some reason I was upset and flustered because she was wearing a blue sailor dress that seemed a little nicer than an everyday going-to-school dress had to be. Plus she was standing so close I could smell the Ivory soap she used to wash her face.

"The instructions said 'a sentence,' and they didn't say it had to be serious! Or even accurate! Or that it couldn't be silly! And why can't Indians not want to live in cottages?" I snatched the paper back so quickly it tore a little in the middle. "Now see what you did!"

Ellen wasn't happy either, but she had a job to do, so she poked a finger at my paper. "The spelling words are all spelled correctly, but these other words aren't. Sister Angelica will take points off for any misspellings in the sentence, not just the assigned words. And you need a comma here and here."

She was about to leave when she thought of something. "And why did you date all the papers April first? Sister Angelica might take off for that, too."

"I do it because this school is one gigantic April Fool's joke."

She sighed, the way very frustrated actors do in movies. "Change them," she said. "To be safe." She turned and stalked into the playground, leaving me standing there like yesterday's bad milk.

Maybe she was fed up enough with me to refuse to help me with my homework anymore. As Sister Regina said, I was the sort of kid who could try the patience of a saint. I didn't actually know why, but the thought of Ellen giving up on me didn't make me feel quite as happy as I might have expected.

The bell rang the moment I stepped into the playground, so I didn't have time to talk with my friends. But Mayor managed to tell me, "We have a plan. The beginning of one, but it could work."

In class, while I was leaning left, then right to avoid detection, Vero was able to fill me in. A little at a time. Every so often, when Angelica was facing away and writing on the blackboard and I was leaning in his direction, he would whisper a phrase or two. "Al the Second Grader" was the first. "Horror comic *The Pit and the Pendulum*" came a minute later. Then, "But instead of a sharp scythe blade we . . ." It felt like forever before he could finish with "have a heavy ball with punji sticks in it. We probably don't need the punji sticks, but you know Al." Angelica turned back to face the class, and all whispered communications ended.

That left me with a picture in my mind. Not much, but something is better than nothing. Just as a little hope for change on day three was better than no hope at all.

A while later, Sister Angelica had us all line up to go to the library. It wasn't a real library, with shelves of books and a librarian. It was an unused classroom, also in the old building down on the first floor, and it had a few dozen dusty old books stacked near the windows. Most of the books had been donated to the school by people cleaning out their basements, and they smelled funny—an aromatic stew of mold, dampness, and rotting glue. Every so often we had to go there to see if we wanted to read any of them.

Out into the dark hall we marched, sixty-two of us in a nice, neat line, according to height, of course. And it was on this journey that I got to dance with a door.

8

Dancing with the Door

I WANT TO SAY right away that *I did not start it.* I did get blamed for it all, but I swear I was innocent. Sort of.

With Sister Angelica in the lead, we headed downstairs to the first floor, marched up the hall, turned right, and proceeded (an extra-credit spelling word that I wasn't able to work into my sentence) down a very long hallway lined with classrooms. The only real light in this hallway came from way at the far end, where there was an intersecting hallway with a bank of windows. I kind of liked the gloomy dark where we were, because it made me feel out of view and safe.

From out of nowhere, Gerald FitzGerald jumped high into the air, did a full twisting circle, landed, and kept on walking as if absolutely nothing unusual had happened. He was taking Irish step-dancing lessons, and he must have felt as invisible as I did.

There were some giggles from kids near Gerry. Sister Angelica must have sensed something with her back-of-the-head vision and supernatural hearing, and she stopped the march to check out what was going on. Since we were all still in a perfect line, she resumed the parade a few seconds later. Which was when Squints jumped, turned in the air, landed, and walked on. He wasn't as graceful as Gerry, but then who is?

Next went Erin (Margaret) O'Connor and a kid named Michael Duffy, both leaping at the same time. It was as if a line of jack-in-the-boxes were blasting from their hiding places and instantly retreating.

When Sister Angelica was almost to the window-lighted hallway where the "library room" was, I jumped as high as I could and tossed my body into an exuberant (another extra-credit word) spin. I don't know why; it seemed like the right thing to do. Only instead of landing and walking on innocently, I made only a three-quarter turn, landed awkwardly, and bumped into Iggy, who, with his tall hair, was right behind me. I stumbled backwards out of the line and across the hall, my arms windmilling wildly.

Our Little League coach once said that hitting a baseball was all about timing. Getting blamed for stuff is also about timing.

As I was staggering backwards, Sister Ursula was opening the door to her fourth-grade classroom. You guessed it. I hit the side of that door with the back of my head so hard that the noise echoed like a bat hitting a ball.

Ordinarily, a student's hitting his (my) head on a two-inch-thick, two-hundred-pound door would result in a nun telling him (me) to be more careful in the future. If you were in enough real pain, sometimes they would forgo additional punishment on top of the blood.

Unfortunately, I whammed that door with so much force that it flew back and smashed Sister Ursula square in the face. She gave out a pathetic, muffled groan, did a back step or two, then toppled to the floor on her rear end. There she was, leaning against the wall, her wire-rimmed glasses hanging from her nose and a clear dent in her forehead and her starched white coif.

You can usually tell how much trouble you are in by the noise level. There was not a sound, not a peep or gasp or anything coming from anyone on line or from Sister Ursula's students. Who were draped over their desks to see what had happened. It was as quiet as a graveyard at midnight, which meant I was doomed.

"What's going on back there?" Sister Angelica shouted, turning and hurrying back down the hallway to where the impact had taken place. Because of the strong backlight from the far end of the hall, she was nothing but a menacing black silhouette getting bigger and bigger, the fabric of her robes and veil flapping madly. She looked like a giant crow coming to peck my eyes out.

Doors along the hall popped open, and three or four nuns stuck their heads out. They looked like curious penguins trying to see who was being attacked by the killer whale.

Sister Angelica looked at Sister Ursula, who was struggling to push herself up. "I'm okay," Sister Ursula mumbled in a faltering voice. "No harm done. No harm. Just a little stunned. Nothing more. Everything will be okay."

She was talking, which meant she was still alive. That was a good sign. But any positive feeling I might have had disappeared when Sister Angelica faced me. I was the only student out of line and undoubtedly the one with the guiltiest look on his face.

She took hold of Sister Ursula's arm, then turned to the line. "Don't just stand there!" she shouted. "Help me get Sister Ursula to her feet. And be careful." I went to help, but Sister Angelica added in a menacing voice, "Not you. You've already done enough." She was breathing very hard, and the look on her face reminded me of Sister Anita's expression just before she stabbed me with her yellow pen.

Sister Ursula was hauled to her feet. She was a little wobbly, but I was glad to see her put her glasses back in place and dust herself off, and I was even happier to hear her say, "Really, it was an accident. I'm fine."

That reassurance made me feel better, but it clearly did not calm Sister Angelica. She was still furious, still taking in deep gulps of air. Both her hands were balled into tight fists and were shaking.

After what felt like an hour, she opened her hands and wiggled her fingers. Then, through clenched teeth, she said in a low growl, "Master Murphy. Go directly to Sister Mary Brian's room and tell her what just happened here." I didn't move immediately, and she spat out, "Now!"

9

I Am the Green Banana

MY MOM TOLD ME that dead people see a bright white light as they head up to heaven. I'm not sure how she knew this, since I don't think she traveled to heaven regularly, but I was willing to believe her. As I walked slowly toward the hallway where the blinding light streamed in, I wondered if there was also light to guide you in the other direction. You know, *down there.* If I ever made it home, I vowed, I'd ask Mom.

When I set off down the hall, I expected Philip to send me off with a farewell message in some language. But he and everyone else were stone-cold quiet. It was that bad. Out of the corner of my eye I saw Roger smirking triumphantly as I passed; then a little ways beyond him I heard a feeble, whispered "Oh, Jimmy." It was Ellen McDonald, and she sounded very disappointed. A few feet later I noticed that Kathy Gathers had turned to watch me march past. Not only was I doomed, but my love for Kathy was probably doomed too.

I felt some relief when I reached the windowed hall, turned right, and was out of sight of the class. I felt the back of my head and found a good-size lump. Not the biggest I'd ever had, but it hurt when I touched it, and when I looked at my fingers, they were covered with blood.

Up this hall I went and through a short transition hall between the old and new parts of the school. Very slowly. No need to rush to my own execution.

Sister Rose Mary's office was just ahead on the left. If I'd been sent there, I'd know what my fate would be: clock-watch time, standing straight for fifteen to thirty minutes, and a lecture. And maybe a poke with her pirate hand. Going to Sister Mary Brian was like entering a pitch-dark cave. If there weren't millions of bats in that cave waiting to get me, there had to be vipers. Or deadly spiders.

Sister Mary Brian's nickname around school was the Enforcer. I never had class with her, so I never saw her in action, but she was rumored to have a spanking machine in her supply closet, as well as a large paddle for mobile punishment. Kids said she could do a lightning-quick grab 'n twist of an ear. When I asked Jerry about her, he looked downright upset and said, "You don't ever want to mess with that one." He hadn't elaborated, but what he told me was enough to make me steer clear of Sister Mary Brian.

I went past the principal's office and the statue of Saint Stephen, crossing myself twice for extra luck. When I reached the door to Sister Mary Brian's second-grade classroom, I knocked extra lightly. If she didn't hear, she might not respond, and then I could wander back to —

"Yes?" I heard her say from inside. "Come in." I wondered if all nuns had to have extremely good hearing as well as back-of-the-head vision before they were admitted to the sisterhood club.

I opened the door and took a step inside. I stared at her, petrified, and didn't say a word. She stared back, her eyebrows narrowing in a questioning way.

"Can I help you, James?" Her knowing who I was and using my first name wasn't necessarily a good thing. It might have been a trap to make me relax and confess everything.

I took a few more steps into the room. All her second graders were quiet and, of course, watching me. I saw a hand make a small waving motion from the middle of the room, and I realized it belonged to Al the Second Grader. Great. An eyewitness to my latest humiliation.

Lying is a sin. You can't miss it because it's right there in black and white in the section of the catechism on mortal and venial sins. But I knew from hearing Uncle Arthur talk about the law that in court there was a lot of gray area between black and white. So I told Sister Mary Brian that Sister Angelica had sent me, and when she asked why, I very carefully said as little as possible. "By accident, I bumped into Sister Ursula's door while she was opening it, and the door hit Sister Ursula."

I left out the part about doing a goofy jump-twist dance that sent me stumbling into the door, and the part about Sister Ursula getting smashed in the face and ending up on her butt. Legally, this might have been labeled a sin of omission. But it was an accident, so technically, I was okay. For the most part.

A flash of inspiration struck. I touched the back of my head and held up my hand for everyone to see. I was happy I hadn't wiped the blood off—every finger was so impressively coated red that several kids gasped. "Sister Ursula is okay," I added. "She said so."

Sister Mary Brian looked confused. I figured she

was trying to sort out how much of my story to believe and how she should deal with me. "Come here, James," she said.

Now, approaching a nun in a situation like this can be tricky. I was clearly guilty of something bad, since I'd been sent there. Even the oldest, most feeble nuns usually still had one lunging pounce left in them — something Sister Anita proved the day she stabbed me. But not going up to Sister Mary Brian might convince her I was lying about everything. So I walked to the front of the classroom. Very cautiously.

Here's the weird thing. I'd always thought Sister Mary Brian was tall. Not Sister Rose Vincent freaky gigantic, but still pretty tall. As I approached her now, I realized she wasn't much taller than I was. I guess I'd spent the last few years avoiding her, so I never noticed she was shrinking.

"Let me see that bump," she ordered when I stopped in front of her. I turned around, and she parted my hair so she could get a good look. "Does this hurt?" she asked, touching the bump.

I cried "Ouch!!!" loud enough, but not too loud, and pulled away a few inches. Too much drama made the nuns suspicious that it was an act, so it was always better to play it down.

"The cut doesn't look very bad," she said calmly. "And you say Sister Ursula is okay?"

"Yes, Sister. She said she was, a few times, and she didn't even seem mad." I paused, thinking I had to admit that I had done something stupid but everyone had survived. "But Sister Angelica was still mad, so she sent me here."

"I see."

That "I see" clearly meant she didn't see at all why I had been sent, if the accident had been as innocent as I'd described it. A few seconds of awkward silence followed. I came within a millisecond of confessing everything, but Sister Mary Brian spoke first.

She turned to face her class. "Children," she said, suddenly cheerful, "I believe that James Murphy here is the answer to our prayers." Me, the answer to someone's prayers? This definitely had to be a mistake. A major one. "James, go stand at the door, please. And children, I want you to line up behind him, and let's keep the chatter to a minimum, shall we?"

Then she added in an unexpectedly happy voice, "I believe we have found our Green Banana!"

10

Chugga-Chugga-Chug

I DID AS DIRECTED and stationed myself at the door. Now what? I wondered. And what was this about me being a green banana? And where were we going, anyway? The kids — all fifty-something of them — piled into a line behind me, girls in front, boys behind, according to height. There was some random whispering going on, and every so often I heard the words "green banana."

"Boys and girls," Sister Mary Brian said over the murmuring, "James will be our locomotive during our walk, and I will be the caboose. You are all passenger cars. James, we're going to the auditorium by way of the back stairway. You should stop at the boys' room to wash your hands."

"Yes, Sister." So I had been a green banana, but

now I was a locomotive. This had to be some sort of torture method they thought up in the convent at night. "I want to hear my chugga-chuggas," she announced, which started my brain thinking, Chugga-chuggas? What the ... But before I could complete that thought, she commanded, "Forward, James."

I started walking, assuming that the short passenger-car folk behind would follow. If they didn't, I intended to keep on walking. All the way home if possible. Almost immediately I heard a chorus of tiny voices behind me chanting, "Chugga-chugga-chug, chugga-chugga-chug." Over and over again. This was bad, of course, but then Sister Mary Brian called out, "And where are my train whistles?"

The phrase *Please shoot me now* entered my brain, but was pushed aside by a series of howling train whistles that nearly drowned out the chugga-chugga-chugs. "Where are my bass whistles?" Sister Mary Brian asked. And guess what? There followed several very low, grumbling "hoot-hoot-hooooots."

I think the floor must have tilted just then. My legs felt a little shaky, and my head just couldn't figure out what was happening. Sister Mary Brian was the Enforcer. She was supposed to have a spanking machine and be ninja quick with the ear grab 'n twist.

But now she had a class marching through school making all sorts of silly sounds. Where had this Sister Mary Brian been during all the years I was avoiding the other, more lethal one?

The line halted for a moment as I ducked into the boys' room and ran cold water over my hands. This time alone helped me to steady myself. When I resumed my locomotive duties, I picked up the pace in self-defense. Best to get where we were going as quickly as possible, and maybe the chugga-chugga-chugs and hoot-hoots would stop.

We passed Saint Stephen's statue, but I didn't bother crossing myself. I didn't need any more of that kind of luck. Though I admit, getting slammed in the head with the rock he had in his hand was looking like a good way to escape all my problems. Which made me realize that most saints are martyrs, and not many martyrs die peacefully in bed.

I was thinking over this martyr thing, wondering why so many seemingly sane people wanted to be a part of that club, as we went up past Sister Rose Mary's office toward the hall with all the windows. This could all be over in a few painful minutes, I assured myself. At this point my heart sank.

My aunt Briana (on the Irish side of our family)

once said that her heart sank when she learned that her no-account first husband, Franky, had emptied their bank account and run off with the bank teller. I didn't think this was possible physically, the heart sinking part. If your heart really did sink, it would cause a real mess inside your body. But I understood exactly what she meant when I passed the principal's office, looked up, and saw Sister Angelica Rose headed in our direction. Trailed by our entire class.

My heart sank all the way to the shiny sky-blue tiled floor. I made eye contact with Sister Angelica for a second, then immediately lowered my gaze to the tiles. Keep moving, I told myself. You can't escape this latest disgrace, not with everyone behind you chugga-chugga-chugging and hoot-hooting so loudly. But getting past my class would at least—

"James," Sister Mary Brian called out. "Please stop the train so I can talk with Sister Angelica for a moment."

I did as directed, my head still down, my eyes taking in the gold speckles in the blue tiles. There must have been a million speckles per square tile, all twinkly and bright. Carefree, even innocent. I wished I could float through the blue vastness to the other side of the universe.

"And children," Sister Mary Brian added, "let's keep the steam up in our boiler, shall we?"

Now instead of chugga-chugga-chugging and hoot-hooting, they began to hiss enthusiastically.

"Hey, Murph. Murph," Vero called in a very low whisper. He wasn't far from me. Maybe fifteen feet or so ahead. "What's going on?" he wanted to know. I wasn't about to say out loud that I was a green banana turned locomotive, so I just shrugged. "Don't worry," Vero said reassuringly. "We'll figure out a plan, and we'll get her."

Several of the guys grumbled, "Yeah, we'll get her." Mayor gave me the thumbs-up, accompanied by nods from Iggy, Tom-Tom, Philip, and Squints. Squints, ever subtle, emphasized his support by making a slashing gesture across his neck and nodding toward Sister Angelica.

By this time I was wondering how the other kids in my class were reacting to my banishment to the second grade. Especially what Kathy Gathers was thinking. But when I glanced around, I saw that Roger Sutternhopf was next to me, his arms crossed across his chest, staring at me.

"James," Sister Mary Brian called out. "Forward to the station!"

Roger gave me what I think might be called an evil sneer. He balled his fists, began moving both arms back and forth slowly, and said just loud enough for me to hear, "Chugga-chugga-chug, chugga-chugga-chug." Other kids near him began to echo his challenge: "Chugga-chugga-chug."

I moved forward, trailed by the passenger cars' innocent chugga-chugga-chugging and hoot-hooting. As I passed the guys, Philip raised his hand as if to say something, then glanced toward Sister Angelica and thought better of it. It would have been nice to have a friendly word from Philip, even if I had no idea what he was saying. Instead he had a kind of *we might never see you again* look on his face.

11

Going Bananas

I TURNED LEFT at the intersection and went up the long hallway, the entire place growing darker as we got farther and farther from the windows. Darker, like the inside of my head.

Sister Angelica was bad enough, but what Roger had done was just . . . just . . . too much. I felt pressure slowly building up inside me, whispering that I had to do something, no matter what, before my head exploded. I didn't remember ever picking on Roger or making fun of him in all our years at St. Stephen's. And I hardly ever said anything bad about him behind his back. There was the pencil box to the head, of course, but even Roger had to know that was an accident. Besides, everyone knew he was smart. I never, ever said he wasn't. So what did the smartest kid in class get out of making fun of the dumbest kid?

I wondered if we could put Roger on the murder-late list along with Sister Angelica, and I was getting a bit of satisfaction from this thought when another intruded. We would be passing Sister Ursula's classroom, and Sister Mary Brian might stop the train again to ask her what really happened.

I ducked my head and held my breath as we passed the door to the fourth-grade room. But there was no command to stop, so I pressed on as quickly as I could without actually breaking into a sprint. Turned the corner and was through the door to the staircase and down in the auditorium a moment later.

All the lights were on, so bright I had to shade my eyes so they could adjust. I started down the wooden stairs that led to the main floor of the auditorium, but Sister Mary Brian called out from behind, "Go straight across the stage, James, and stop at the other side."

I was halfway across the stage when I noticed Bernie, the janitor. He was perched high on a tall, wobbly wooden ladder, way backstage, where they stored lights, stage props for class shows, boxes, and pieces of dusty old furniture. When Sister Mary Brian appeared, Bernie called out, "If you want, I can come back later to do this, Sister." He took a step down the ladder, which leaned dangerously left and right, left and right.

"No, no, no, Bernie. You finish what you're doing. You aren't in our way at all." She walked to the center of the stage, then added, "And you know that Sister Angelica needs the bowling alleys as soon as possible. We don't want to disappoint her, now, do we?"

Alleys? Sister Angelica needed the alleys? Then I remembered. When the school was built, way back in like 1935, they put two bowling alleys in the backstage area. They also lined the walls of the auditorium with basketball hoops. After school, any nun who wanted could come from the convent, which was about twenty feet from the side door of the auditorium, and bowl her heart out. I couldn't picture the nuns shooting baskets, so I assumed the hoops were for kids. The bowling alleys hadn't been used in years, and even though there were lots of boxes and chairs on them, I could see dirt and dust coating the wood, plus several loose planks sticking up.

"No, Sister," Bernie called down. "But I think I might have bad news for her. I have to sand and recoat the wood to make it smooth, and it'll take at least a week for it to dry proper."

"Well, in that case—" Sister Mary Brian began,

but then she changed gears. "Well, that's all the more reason you should continue with your work there, isn't it?"

"Yes, Sister." He went back up the swaying ladder and began winding up the fifteen or twenty long cords used to hold up painted scene panels.

I didn't have much time to think about the bowling alleys or why Angelica wanted them. Sister Mary Brian ordered all her Yellow Bananas to get into position. In a matter of seconds they formed a giant V, which she called the Victory-V. The group named the Banana Boat kids were told to stand stage right. I was puzzling over this reference to Banana Boat kids when she had another group move to stage left. They also seemed to be fruit related. I assumed that this rehearsal was for the pre-Thanksgiving show, where the kindergarten through fifth-grade classes sang and danced for their parents. Maybe Sister Mary Brian liked fruit cocktail.

I was all set. The entire class was positioned for the rehearsal and waiting patiently, so my job was officially done. "Ah, Sister," I ventured. I raised my hand tentatively. "Maybe I should go back to my class now?"

I had chosen my words and tone of voice very,

very carefully. I didn't want her to think I was demanding to be released or even implying that it was time she let me go. Better to make a gentle suggestion and let her find the right answer on her own. Only she didn't.

"Go? Now?" She didn't seem upset or annoyed. Only a little confused. "Sister Angelica said I could have you for the rest of the afternoon. We have a lot of territory to cover here today."

I might have groaned, but I probably did it very quietly. You never want to let a nun know you're annoyed or impatient. There is simply no way to win that contest.

"And James, why don't you take your position at the head of the Yellow Bananas." Sister Mary Brian pointed to the spot at the very front of the Victory-V. "Where the Green Banana stands."

My position? The situation was starting to look very complicated. Not to mention inescapable. And it was Sister Angelica who had sentenced me to this torture.

I stood where directed, and then Sister Mary Brian announced, "I haven't written the lyrics yet, but we can all hum the tune and dance." She said this while descending to the floor of the auditorium, where a beat-up black upright piano sat. After settling on the bench, she raised both hands in the air, ready to pounce on the piano keys. "On three. One . . . and two . . ."

"Ah, Sister," I said loudly to get her attention. Once again I raised my hand.

"Yes?"

"I can't dance." It was very quiet all of a sudden, except for a few giggles from the Yellow Bananas behind me.

"Can't dance?"

"No. I can hum, if that helps."

"You'll be doing the box step. Everybody can do the box step. You do know the box step, don't you?"

I said no, and a frustrated Sister Mary Brian jumped to her feet and charged back up the stairs to the stage.

It had happened at last. Sister Mary Brian had tossed aside her good-nun act and turned back into the Enforcer, ready to nail me for having no dancing ability. I almost welcomed the coming assault, as it would reaffirm my view of the world of St. Stephen's.

But she didn't hit me or even grab and twist my ear. Instead, she swooped in next to me, and I was immediately surrounded by the heavy smell of baby powder. "The box step is easy," she told me. "Here, watch my feet." She hiked up the hem of her long robe and dangled her left foot, with its shiny sensible black shoe and six or seven inches of her ankle, out front for me to watch. Oh my, I thought.

She kept talking and even took a step forward, but I wasn't paying any attention. None. Seeing a nun's shoe is one thing, but seeing her ankle is another story altogether. And probably a sin. The smell of baby powder was making it hard for me to breathe.

I'd seen enough shows on TV to know that stages usually had trapdoors where actors could appear and disappear in seconds. I hoped a door would open beneath me and I could fall into the empty black space below.

"James, are you paying attention?"

I told her no (better to be honest) and that I was thinking about something (though I failed to mention that I was thinking about being dropped into the black abyss of the fiery underworld for seeing her ankle). I shook my head to clear it of these thoughts.

"Now, watch closely. It's really very simple." She took a step forward with her left foot and planted it on the stage floor. Next, she brought her right foot forward, touched the side of her left foot with it, then slid her right foot a step to the right, planted it, and slid her left foot over next to it. "That's half the box," she pointed out. "Now we do it backwards." She took a step back with her right foot, planted it, brought the left foot back, touched the side of the right foot, then stepped to the left with her left foot, ending by bringing over the right foot so it was right next to the left. "Simple, right?"

Well, no, not really. But she didn't wait for my answer. Instead, she repeated the box-step demonstration and made me follow along step by step next to her. Each time we did it, she went a little faster and another gust of baby powder assaulted me. Then she began humming what I guessed was the tune to the Yellow Bananas' song.

I needed to get away from her. For years, she had been the Enforcer, an evil, dangerous presence, ever ready to strike. But she had now suddenly turned bizarrely nice. Or just weird. Didn't matter; neither made sense. I mean, she was dancing and humming and altogether not what I thought she would be. Which only made me suspicious. She had to revert for real at some point, the way seemingly normal people turn into werewolves when the moon is full.

Then I had a revelation. If I learned the box step

well enough, she'd be able to ignore me and focus on her chorus of fruits. So I really tried to concentrate and do the steps as directed. A few minutes later my strategy was working, and she hurried back to the piano.

Once again she called out, "One . . . and two . . . and three!" At which point she hit those piano keys so hard that my ears started to buzz. She was beating on the keys as if she were wearing boxing gloves, but I have to admit, she played with real gusto. "Gusto" was a word my dad used when describing musicians who could play a tune with extreme enthusiasm.

We did our dance nine or ten times. Then the Banana Boat kids took center stage while we stood on the sidelines. Because the stage was oven warm and I was wearing a long-sleeved shirt, I was sweating bullets just standing there. After the Banana Boat kids came the third group, which also turned out to be about bananas. They did a song where the word "banana" was rhymed with all sorts of made-up words, like "fo-fana," "bo-bana," and "hold-hammer" (though the last was pronounced *hold-hamma*).

Here is where my brain stepped in again and took over. While the other groups did their songs, my mind drifted to questions like, What is my class doing right now? Why did Sister Angelica have to do this to me? Is Kathy Gathers thinking about me? And What made Sister Mary Brian decide that bananas were a food group worth singing and dancing about? Then I glanced up at Bernie, who was still way up near the rafters, tucking in those long cords so they didn't dangle down onto the decrepit bowling alleys.

Maybe, I thought as I watched, Sister Angelica wanted to bowl after school for exercise, which was fine. She might take out her eternal annoyance on the pins instead of me and Philip. I saw a rope slip from Bernie's hand and begin swinging back and forth, back and forth. It was at this exact moment that I figured out how we could murderlate Sister Angelica Rose.

12
Absolutely Genius

I WASN'T RELEASED from my banana box-step bondage until the dismissal bell rang. I hurried to the exit door, hoping I could catch up to Mayor or Iggy or somebody and tell them what I'd come up with. But naturally, Sister Mary Brian had a parting comment before I could disappear up the stairs.

"James, our next rehearsal will be on Thursday."

I stopped dead in my tracks and spun around. "Next Thursday?" But ... but ... Sister Ursula was okay. She said so herself. And technically, the door slam was an accident. One afternoon of box-step torture was plenty of punishment, wasn't it?

"Yes, Thursday afternoon. I've already spoken to Sister Angelica. I'll send one of my students to get you." She turned around to organize her class train to chugga-chugga-chug back to their classroom. Al gave me a quick wave, but I was too shocked by my extended sentence to wave back.

Up the stairs I flew. I was about to dash out through a side door to catch up with the guys, but I stopped when I realized that I didn't have any books. Once I left the building, I might not be able to get back inside. All the doors locked when they closed, and the main entrances were guarded by suspicious nuns who could say *No, you can't come back inside,* especially to someone (me) who was instantly a suspect and had a red folder with his (my) name on it.

In the past I would have just left and not worried about books. But I remembered Ellen and our seven o'clock call. I'd already disappointed her once today and didn't want to hear that in her voice again. So here I was, thinking about doing something to make Ellen happy, which was all so complicated and confusing I didn't think I could stand any more. I pushed this aside, sighed, and let the door swing shut before heading up the stairs to our classroom.

The room was empty of kids, as expected. Not expected was Sister Angelica Rose sitting at her desk, head down, marking papers.

Run! was my first thought, along with sensations of panic, fear, and trembling. She hadn't looked up from the papers (maybe her magical radar was turned off). I could probably slip away down the dark hall unobserved. I heard Sister Rose Mary's bell ringing far away and was immediately envious of the kids she was trying to silence — mainly because they were heading out of the building to freedom.

Sister Angelica stopped writing for a second and rubbed her eyes with two fingers. My dad did this when his eyes were tired after a long day of studying clients' ledger books. Sister Angelica closed her eyes briefly and shook her head gently before going back to her marking. So I was still unnoticed and could escape. But I needed to grab some books so I could have something to talk about with Ellen. Maybe I could tiptoe in quietly and get my books without Sister Angelica even knowing.

This, of course, was a bogus idea and guaranteed to fail from the start. Her ability to see things going on behind her and hear the faintest whisper might have turned on again. But, I reasoned, if I tried to be quiet and she knew I was trying, she might let me zip in and out without much abuse. So I took the softest, quietest, most delicate step ever, and immediately caught my toe on the raised oak door saddle. The next thing I knew, I was lunging into the room, my feet slapping down as if I were wearing big, floppy clown shoes. This was not my day for moving gracefully, that was for sure.

Sister Angelica sat up abruptly and dropped her pencil, clearly startled. "What . . ." she gasped. Then she realized it was me. "Oh."

"I need to get my books," I explained when I'd stopped stumbling. I pointed to my desk, as if she didn't know where I sat.

Sister Angelica nodded. "And James," she added. She must have been very tired or distracted because she didn't "Master Murphy" me. She picked up her pencil and pointed over her shoulder to the blackboard. "I put tonight's assignments on the board, so you might want to take a minute to copy them down." Then she went back to her work.

So there I was, in a hot, empty classroom, me at my little metal desk and Sister Angelica at her big wooden one. The only sound came from our pencils scritch-scratching across paper—me squinting to see the board and desperately scribbling the assignments down while she scanned her papers like a sniper ready to pounce on each and every enemy mistake. We were kind of like armies facing each other across a no man's land of shiny desks, waiting for the next battle to begin.

I finished, gathered up my books, and started to leave. Quietly. In a few seconds I would be out of there and free again. I was halfway to the door when I suddenly had this odd feeling. Like I shouldn't just leave without saying something to Sister Angelica. My parents were always telling me to be as polite as possible, especially to older people and teachers.

"Ah, good afternoon, Sister."

She didn't look up. "Good afternoon, James." Her voice sounded as dry as dead leaves and about as enthusiastic. I had almost reached the door when she swiveled in her chair to face me, holding up a paper. "And could you put the correct date on your papers from now on?"

"Yes, Sister."

Then I bolted out of the room.

Once in the hallway, I raced — down the stairs, out a door, over to where the guys sometimes hang out after school. Only everyone was gone. But I had news — a plan — an idea about how we could finally murderlate-embarrass Sister Angelica, and I had to tell somebody. Soon, or I might burst.

Then it came to me. Philip. He might be home, and for obvious reasons he was an especially good listener. So I double-quick headed for home, passing by the corner store and my usual salty potato sticks, even though I was hungry from all that box-step stuff. I was on a mission and wanted to get it moving forward as quickly as possible.

I started thinking about how we could use the swinging cord on the stage. I didn't think up many — any, actually — details, but I wanted to be able to describe what might happen so that somebody else could cook up the technical stuff.

I was thinking about this and really excited. I didn't deserve what had happened to me on the first or second or third day of school. In fact, I didn't deserve a lot of the things that had happened to me at St. Stephen's over the years. But now I might be able to settle the score, as Squints might put it.

I was hurrying across the train bridge, head down, when I heard, "Hey, handsome. In too much of a hurry to say hello?"

It was the three high school girls in their short plaid skirts and tight sweaters. I'd almost blown right past them, I was so consumed by my racing thoughts. I pointed lamely in the general direction of home and even glanced that way for a second, then looked back at them. "I have to tell a friend something."

"Oh," said the brunette with the red sweater.

"What's your name, anyway? We were just wondering."

Why would they be wondering what my name was? I really didn't care, since having them ask was flattering. "Um, Jimmy," I answered. And realized instantly that it made me sound as if I were all of seven years old. I gave a little throat-clearing cough and lowered my voice. "Jim. Jim Murphy."

"You're kidding me, right?" This was said by the girl with a yellow and black plaid skirt and yellow sweater. "My dad's John MacGullion. MacGullion Heating and Air Conditioning. His accountant's name is Jim Murphy. Are you related?"

"Yeah, he's my dad. He's a CPA. A certified public accountant. That's different from just an accountant." Now why did I go and say that? I wondered. I mean, she was trying to be nice, and there I went telling her she didn't know what she was talking about.

"I didn't know that, Jim Murphy Jr., but I'll remember it now." She was smiling nicely. "You have a great day." And the three continued along Kearny Avenue.

I watched them wander off, wondering what the encounter meant. If it meant anything. Then I turned and rushed toward home. It sounded like they were flirting with me, kind of, but why would pretty high school girls bother with me? I didn't think they were trying to make fun of me either. I was pretty good at sensing when people were doing that. It was a little confusing, really, but a lot of things in life are confusing. Such as, why couldn't Kathy Gathers try to flirt with me?

My shirt was wringing wet by the time I got home and put my books on the stairs leading to the second floor. I went to the kitchen and was surprised to see that the table had been moved against the wall and the swastika was gone, leaving an irregular shape of raw wood

The night before, I had watched Dad get his Pepsi from the refrigerator and stop on his way to the living room to stare at the red tiles. He grimaced and shook his head before leaving to have his nightly soda.

He must have gotten tired of seeing the swastika and thinking about the kind of club meetings that might have taken place in our kitchen. He had come home at lunchtime and ripped up all the red tiles and some of the green tiles around them, just to get them out of his sight. A flat-edge ice chopper was leaning against the wall, and the ripped-up tiles were packed in five brown A&P grocery bags lined up next to it.

I went to the back window and looked across at Philip's bedroom window. His room was dark and gloomy, so he always put on his reading lamp when he was in there studying his foreign-language books. No light was visible now.

I was becoming very frustrated. I don't usually have good ideas, not like, say, Mayor or Iggy. Or any other kid in our class, really. I wanted to tell somebody and find out if I really had a decent idea.

I could wait at the kitchen window for Philip's light to go on, but that might take hours. What to do?

I was pretty sure Dad wanted to rip up the entire floor, so he might actually appreciate it if I took up some of the green tiles. I grabbed the ice chopper and started scraping up the tiles surrounding the exposed raw wood underfloor. Dad had left four empty paper bags on a chair, and I filled them pretty quickly.

I went to the back window, but Philip's light still wasn't on. Now what? I knew. I grabbed up forks, spoons, knives, and everything else, and I set the dining room table. We probably wouldn't be eating in the kitchen until the new floor was in, so this seemed like a natural thing to do. When I finished setting the table, Philip *still* wasn't in his room. Where was he, anyway?

By this time I was a ball of nervous energy. I couldn't get done what I wanted to get done, namely tell someone — anyone — what I'd thought up. I ran the idea through my brain a few dozen times and decided it was more than just decent, even more than good. It was absolutely genius. I paced around a little, going from the kitchen to the dining room to the living room and back to the kitchen. Still no Philip.

I knew I was desperate because on my fourth journey through the rooms I scooped up my books and sat down at the kitchen table. Yes, I started on my homework, checking between assignments to see if Philip was home.

About an hour later Philip's light went on and I scooted out to talk to him. His window was open, and I could hear music coming from his room. In addition to reading books about foreign languages, Philip sometimes listened to a station that played Italian operas.

I leaned over the low fence between our yards and knocked on Philip's window. He said "Hey," and I immediately launched into telling him about my idea. It came out in a gulp and garble of words that would have made Erin (Margaret) O'Connor proud. I mentioned the bowling alleys and how Sister Angelica would be using them, the long cords that Bernie had been tucking in, and Al the Second Grader's mention of *The Pit and the Pendulum*. Then I told him my genius idea. "We could use one of the cords, see, and have a ball on the end, and when she throws a bowling ball, it swings down and bam!, right in the kisser." I was very proud of myself. "So, do you think it'll work?"

Instead of saying yes, it was the most brilliant idea he'd ever heard, Philip looked thoughtful for a second. In the background a female was singing her heart out in Italian, and it sounded as if someone were strangling her. Then he said, "H . . . h . . . how? Th . . . the . . . de . . . de . . . tails?"

I told him I hadn't come up with any details, but hoped he or Iggy or Mayor or the other guys might figure that stuff out. He nodded slowly, and I realized that I wanted him — or anybody — to say it wasn't the dumbest idea ever. Positive feedback can feel good, after all. "So, do you think we can figure this out and murderlate Angelica once and for all?"

Philip leaned forward and whispered, *"Il tiranno sara rovesciate da mani di molte persone buone."*

The Italian singer must have finally died, because suddenly the singing stopped and an eerie quiet surrounded me. I was certain that every neighbor was listening, so I lowered my voice. "Phil, what does that mean? Do you think my idea can work?"

Philip leaned in even closer to the window screen. "Th . . . th . . . the tyrant can . . . b . . . b . . . be top . . . top . . . toppled b . . . by . . . by th . . . th . . . the hands of . . . of . . . of many good pee . . . pee . . ." He took a gulp of air and finished, "many good people."

I figured that was Philip's way of saying yes.

13

Plausible Deniability

TIME FLIES WHEN you're having fun. At least that's what my mom always said. She usually added, "So make sure you always have fun. But not too much." Not having too much fun was very easy to do at St. Stephen's.

Anyway, the amazing thing is that my time-flying fun started right after I came back from chatting with Philip. We were at dinner when Dad suddenly said, "I took up the red kitchen tiles, and I'm wondering who ripped up the green ones."

Jerry immediately pointed across the table at me with his fork and announced, "I didn't do it. He did!"

This was an understandable reaction. Better to place blame for a crime as soon as possible and not get caught up in the investigation. I said, "Yeah, I did. I thought you wanted to get rid of them."

"I do," Dad said. He snapped his fingers as if he'd just had a brainstorm (even though it was obvious he'd been thinking about it for a while). "I have an idea. Why don't you rip up and bag all the rest of the tiles? I'll pay you a dollar a bag. I brought a bunch of bags home tonight."

Jerry quickly put in, "I can do that too," but Dad shook his head gently and said, "No, no, that's okay, Jerry. Jimmy started the job, so he should finish it."

"But I want to make some money too," Jerry pleaded, and here's where my day got even better. For me, anyway.

My mom said, "I know. I'll give you a dollar to clean the oven."

"You mean I have to stick my head in a disgusting oven for a buck?"

I was tempted to say something snotty, but I didn't—not a word to rub in Jerry's attempt to blame me. Which was unusual for me.

Mom managed to make my night even better when she suggested that if Jerry didn't want to clean the oven, he could spread manure around the garden. "The roses need a good feeding before winter. And you can deadhead them, too."

Jerry looked clueless about this last part, so Mom

explained. "Deadheading means cutting off the dead flowers."

"Oh," was Jerry's response, followed by, "How much do I get for each deadhead?"

Even school got a little better in the following days. I leaned left, then right, just enough that Sister Angelica didn't bother me at all. Still, she kept calling on Philip and making him answer questions in English, so that his cheeks and ears always seemed to blaze a red glow. I managed to get most of my homework done and even got a 75 on a spelling quiz, thanks to Ellen's constant calls, prodding, badgering, and advice. Only the scores weren't read out loud, so Kathy Gathers never knew that I'd improved on my 30 percent grade.

I had to go to the auditorium on Thursday to practice being the Green Banana, but even that wasn't so bad. Well, it wasn't a lot of fun, but I kind of liked it when I came onstage and one of the Yellow Bananas whispered, "The Green Banana is here to save the day!" Have to admit I felt a little like a superhero, there to save a fruit cup.

Apart from bananas, conditions in the auditorium got better and better. Bernie moved all the stuff from the bowling alleys to the very back of the stage and piled it as high as he could lift things. Next, he nailed down all the bowling alley boards, sanded both alleys, and put some sort of finishing lacquer on them. But the weather got hotter and hotter and the humidity went up and up, so the coating never dried. It was always sticky when he touched it. And it stank like airplane glue, so no one was allowed in the auditorium for more than a week.

Finally Bernie decided he must have used the wrong finish on the bowling alleys, and he had to sand it off and start all over again. Which meant another week of not being the Green Banana while the alleys dried and the stink disappeared. Two whole weeks without having to do a box step. God really does work in mysterious ways, and sometimes the results ended up good for me.

During this time, the Plan to murderlate Sister Angelica was moving forward. Philip had told the guys what I'd said through the screen, and Mayor took it from there. By the time I found them in the playground — Ellen had waylaid me to talk about my math problems, my spelling-word sentences, and my geography map drawing, none of which I seemed to have done perfectly — the Plan was pretty much in place.

Mayor, Iggy, Squints, and Tom-Tom were going to volunteer to help Bernie clean up the auditorium stage. Bernie had decided that the stuff being stored backstage had to be cleared out completely before the bowling alleys could be used. He worried that kids might bump into something and break it. Bernie had been grumbling about how much work it would be to move all of it, especially in the humid heat, so Mayor thought he'd be more than happy to have some help. This would give Iggy a chance to study the long cords hanging up in the rafters to see if we could rig a pendulum-like trap.

"I can help too," I said. I wanted to actually take part in putting this all together.

Mayor shook his head no. "Plausible deniability, Murph. You need to stay clear."

"Plausible what?"

"Deniability," Mayor repeated. "When this happens, who's going to be blamed first?"

I knew the answer perfectly well but managed to hesitate a beat or two. "*You* will be blamed," Mayor continued. He gave me the hard look a sergeant might give a dopey recruit, and he poked me in the chest with a finger. "You need to go to rehearsals, do whatever you're doing there, and get out without ever showing any interest in the bowling alleys. None. When you're blamed—and you will be—Mary Brian, Bernie, and all those other kids will have to say you never once went near the cords or even mentioned them."

"You'll be home free," Iggy tossed in.

It's very hard to argue with such logic, so I said okay.

Meanwhile, Vero was going to round up some old cloth bags his grandfather had. The idea was that we would fill one with flour, and it would swing down and nail Sister Angelica the first time she went bowling. The only one not happy with the new Plan was Al the Second Grader. He was hoping we would change our minds about his punji sticks. "Listen, Al, there's no way to secure them in the flour," Iggy told him. "And like we said before, maybe they're a bit of an overkill, if you get what I mean."

Al didn't quite get it, but I did. The Bible says "an eye for an eye," right? So maybe assault by punji sticks was a little over-the-top, considering that Angelica hadn't actually drawn blood from either Philip or me. Not yet, anyway.

My life at school was sailing along amazingly well. Sister Angelica wasn't bothering me, I was doing a little better with my schoolwork, the Green Banana rehearsals were on hold (and I hoped the whole thing might disappear if enough time went by), and the Plan was moving ahead. This was great, I told myself. I almost looked forward to going to school.

Then Sister Jane came for a visit, and the fun times ended.

14

You Are So Dead

ONE DAY A COUPLE of weeks later, schoolwork was going along smoothly. I was beginning to relax and —instead of always being tense and on my guard and trying to hide behind Joey—even listen to what Sister Angelica was trying to teach us.

On the day of Sister Jane's visit, Sister Angelica seemed nervous and snappy. She barked at Philip when he was trying to answer in English, which wasn't fair and only made him blush and stammer more. And she said something mildly sarcastic to Mary Claire Danes, who was one of the good-smart kids.

At ten o'clock in the morning there was a gentle knock on the classroom door. Sister Angelica looked up, smiled, and headed toward the door, announcing, "Our guest is here, class. Let's all be on our best behavior, shall we?"

In walked Sister Jane, who immediately got everybody's attention for a number of reasons. First off, she was just plain Sister Jane. Not Sister Jane Marie Rose or some such. Second, she wasn't wearing a nun's habit—the first time we'd seen a nun in regular clothes. She had on baggy beige pants with big pockets and a billowy light green shirt that wasn't buttoned all the way up at the neck. The only item that might have been taken as religious was her brown beanie cap, which had a white stripe that ran front to back and another that ran side to side. It looked like one of the hot cross buns my mom made around Easter. One that had been left in the oven a little too long.

"This is our friend Sister Jane," Sister Angelica told us, "and she is visiting all the way from Hawaii, where she works with people who have leprosy."

A little buzz ran through the class. We'd all seen movies about lepers and how they were sometimes sent away from their families so they wouldn't infect anyone with the disease. Which was pretty awful, according to every movie I'd seen about lepers. Apparently, leprosy made body parts fall off.

The third reason she had our attention was because she was black. Now, Kearny is right next to Newark, where lots of black families lived. And there were black people living in our town, though they were mostly down by the meadowlands near the factories. I sometimes went along with Dad when he worked on the books for his clients over there. I got to hang around in the factory tool shops and where the injection mold machines were running, and a lot of the workers were black men and women. So it wasn't as if I'd never encountered a black person before.

But there were only two black kids at St. Stephen's that I knew of, and not many went to St. Stephen's Church, which was about a mile to the north. Most of the black people who were Catholic and lived in Kearny went to the church down near Harrison Park. A black nun named Jane who worked with lepers was pretty unusual in these parts.

Sister Jane thanked Sister Angelica for the nice introduction and then said hello to the class. We replied with a bellowing chorus of "Good morning, Sister Jane."

"Well, Sister Angelica is correct," she said. "I do work with people who have a disease, though nowadays we don't say they have leprosy. We say they have Hansen's disease." She paused a second while we all took this in. Then she smiled. "The disease is named after Gerhard Armauer Hansen, a doctor from Norway who discovered its cause in 1873 . . ."

She told us more about Hansen's disease, and though I heard parts of what she said, I found myself distracted. When she smiled, I saw that she wasn't very old, unlike every nun I'd encountered. Maybe twenty-two or twenty-three. And her sparkling dark eyes seemed very friendly. Maybe even mischievous. She clearly didn't mind shocking us a little with gruesome details.

She had a gold ring on her right hand that looked like a wedding ring. Everyone I knew who had a wedding ring wore it on the left hand. So I looked at her left hand, which she was holding at her side. It took a moment to fully absorb what I'd just seen, and here is where my brain once again betrayed me.

My hand shot up before I could even tell myself not to raise it. I might even have gulped in air and waved my hand back and forth the way a lot of the annoying good-smart kids did when they wanted to make a teacher notice them.

"James." That was Sister Angelica, and the way she said my name was meant to be a warning not to do or say anything stupid.

"That's okay," Sister Jane said to Sister Angelica. She turned to me. "Do you have a question?"

I stood up and only then realized I was really nervous. Standing up made me an easy target. "Yes, Sister. I saw you have a ring on your right hand. Is that a wedding ring? I mean nuns can't get married, but it kinda looks like a wedding ring."

There was an interested mumble from everyone in the class as they leaned forward to see the ring. Sister Angelica frowned and said, "James." This time her tone suggested that I had just asked the silliest question in history.

"No, that's all right," Sister Jane responded. "I am asked that question a lot." She explained that the ring was a gift from her parents when she took her vows as a nun. "It reminds me of them when I'm far away and lonely. And it reminds me that I chose a certain kind of work, and that I want to be very good at that job. You could say I'm married to my work."

"Thank you, James." Sister Angelica stared at me. It wasn't really a *Thank you for that thoughtful question* so much as a *Now sit down and be quiet.*

But I kept going. "I have another question, Sister Jane." Sister Jane nodded, and even though nervous sweat rolled down my back, I went on. "I know you help people with Handsome disease . . ."

The class erupted with laughter, Sister Jane kind of smiled, and Sister Angelica said, "James!!!" Which was very easy to interpret. When the kids quieted down, I continued. "I mean Hansen's disease. So I know you work with them, and I wondered if that's why you're missing a finger on your left hand."

If you thought my Handsome disease slip got a loud response, you should have heard the absolute uproar after the missing finger question. Followed by chaos, bedlam, and pandemonium. It was so deafening I couldn't even hear what sort of "James" Sister Angelica howled.

Sister Jane flashed a huge smile and held up her left hand for everyone to see. Now kids were jumping to their feet to get a look, some of them groaning and moaning. Most of us were just studying her hand, fascinated.

When everyone finally stopped chattering and sat down, Sister Jane said very pleasantly, "It's a myth that people with Hansen's disease lose body parts. My missing finger has nothing to do with the work I do now." She lowered her hand to her side. "I lost it when

I was twelve while driving a tractor on my parents' farm in Michigan."

She went on to tell us about the different jobs she did on the farm and how the accident had happened. As she talked, kids began to lose interest in her missing finger. I don't know about them, but I was amazed that a twelve-year-old girl could drive a tractor by herself and do all kinds of really hard jobs on a farm, like plowing gigantic fields, stringing barbed wire, and killing chickens when they stopped laying eggs. Then she started telling us about her work in Hawaii, and that sounded even harder—teaching kids who had the disease, caring for the elderly and sick patients, and even helping to build the community hospital. I had to admit, she was one really cool Sister of Charity.

I was actually starting to feel proud that I'd asked my questions, since they seemed to have gotten everybody jazzed up and listening. Maybe even Kathy Gathers had been impressed. And then Vero whispered, "Murph. You are so dead."

Like everybody else, I had been riveted by Sister Jane's talk and not paying attention to anything else. But I knew perfectly well that Vero was suggesting I turn my attention to a brewing hurricane called Angelica. I glanced at Sister Angelica, whose face had contorted and turned a dark, burning, furious purple. Made all the more angry-looking because it contrasted so sharply with the starched white rectangular cardboard coif that locked in her face. As soon as we made eye contact, she mouthed, "See me at lunchtime."

I had been standing all this time. Now I slowly sank back into my seat and wished I had Hansen's disease. At least then I could have hidden away in Hawaii.

15

Well, He's Gone and Done It Again

SISTER JANE FINISHED her chat at 11:15 and then went to visit some other classrooms. I had forty-five minutes to stew about my upcoming demise.

Mostly I didn't think I'd done anything particularly wrong. Sure, pointing out that Sister Jane had a missing finger was, well, startling, but she didn't seem to mind. And everybody in class was okay with it. Oh, and I think we all learned a lot more because we were suddenly more focused. So everybody was good with my questions. Except Sister Angelica.

I started wishing that my uncle Arthur were here to defend me. A lot of kids—Mayor, Iggy, Kathy Gathers, Mary Claire Danes, Roger Sutternhopf, for example—were able to explain themselves very clearly, especially if a teacher challenged them for some reason. I usually sputtered and said something lame, like "Yeah, well, um, I really didn't mean to" and other unconvincing babble. Mostly because I knew that I'd been judged guilty even before the evidence was presented. So I needed a good mouthpiece.

At noon Sister Angelica told me to stay put and said she'd be back in a few minutes. Then she led the class down to the cafeteria.

It's funny how you can hear every sound in an empty, quiet classroom. The big clock on the wall ticking. The windows rattling every time a gust of wind blows past. A door slamming on the floor below. The other amazing thing is how small a sixth grader can feel in an empty classroom.

Sister Angelica came back five minutes later. Her face wasn't as dark and hard as before, but her cheeks were flushed and both her hands were tightly balled up. It was clear she was still massively teed off.

"I have never, *EVER*, been so . . . so . . . embarrassed, humiliated, so . . . so . . ."

I wished Uncle Arthur were sitting with me, so he could jump to his feet and proclaim loudly, *We strongly object, Your Honor! Sister Angelica was not the object of my nephew's — ah, my client's — questions, and she has no reason or right to be embarrassed.*

As you can tell, I also wished there were a judge handy. One who hadn't read my red MURPHY folder.

"The wedding ring question was bad enough," Angelica went on, "but pointing out Sister Jane's . . . ah . . . finger! It was mortifying and completely inappropriate . . ."

Uncle Arthur: *Once again, Your Honor, we object! Sister Jane did not seem at all upset. In fact, she smiled at my client after each question was asked.*

"And your . . . your . . . your questions upset the class . . ."

Uncle Arthur: *Objection! The two questions made the class more attentive to Jane's responses and, I might point out, prompted a lively interchange of ideas and additional questions.*

"I don't know how I'm going to face Sister Jane tonight or what to say . . ."

Of course I did not say anything in my own defense and only responded with "Yes, Sister" five times, "No, Sister" once (when she wanted to know if I'd asked the missing finger question on purpose to embarrass Sister Jane), and "I'm sorry, Sister" twice. She said a lot more, going over the same territory in several different tones of voice. Why is it that some adults don't think kids can hear and remember something they said the first time, so they feel compelled to repeat it ten times? But I had tuned out, since I pretty much knew what she was going to say. She ended a lifetime later by telling me to take out a piece of lined paper and write "I will not embarrass a guest in our class ever again." One hundred times. "And make sure every sentence is done neatly, or you'll be doing it all over again!"

Uncle Arthur: *We object, Your . . .* I stopped cold before my thought-objection was complete. One hundred times was easy. Compared with, say, Sister Anita's written punishments—she seemed to really love the number five hundred. But the punishment was still completely unfair—and was all Sister Angelica's doing!

Sister Angelica pulled out her chair with a loud thump, sat down aggressively, and let out a frustrated grunt. I got out my three-ring binder and a sharp pencil and began writing.

I wrote the sentence, making sure to number it. Then I wrote another. And another. Every so often I'd tell myself to write as carefully as possible and make sure every word was spelled correctly. Because the space between the lines was small, I decided to skip a line after each sentence. This made it look a lot better, but I was really eating up paper.

At sentence number 37, my fingers began cramping up in a painful ball. I shook my hand to loosen it, blew on it a few times, and decided a brief rest was in order.

The first thing I wondered was whether I could tape three pencils together in a line so every time I wrote, I would do three sentences at once. I didn't have any tape, and I doubted if Sister Angelica would lend me any from the supply closet, so I abandoned this creative notion as hopeless.

Next I wondered what the rest of the kids in my class were thinking about me. Did any of them feel that I'd been picked on unfairly? And if so, was one of them Kathy Gathers? That was possible and would make missing lunch and having a cramped hand bearable.

I started writing again, but after just five more sentences my hand cramped up. So I looked out the window and spotted eight or nine blackbirds sitting side by side on a telephone wire. They seemed to be staring in at me and shaking their little heads in disappointment. As if they were murmuring to each other, *Well, he's gone and done it again, hasn't he? What a loser.*

Uncle Arthur: *Objection!*

The birds suddenly flew off in alarm with a great flapping of wings and squawking. Well, one "objection" had worked, and I actually chuckled out loud at the notion.

"You should be writing your sentences," Sister Angelica muttered darkly, "and not wasting time."

"Yes, Sister."

I finished up sentence number 100 a minute before lunch ended, and I showed the pages to Sister Angelica. She frowned at them, scanned them quickly, then told me to stay where I was while she went to round up the class. My stomach growled with hunger, but I had a feeling that starving through the afternoon had been added to my penance.

The class came filing in — girls first, boys following, all according to height, of course. For one second, they looked like a jury bringing in a guilty verdict. But that thought passed when I saw that most of the kids weren't staring at me to see if I'd suffered too much or not enough. Ellen and Kathy each tossed me a quick glance, but hardly anyone else seemed to notice I was there.

Except the guys.

In they came toward the end of the procession, looking very determined, and sat down without saying more than "Hey." But a few minutes into the afternoon, when Sister Angelica was writing on the board,

[131]

Vero reached over and handed me a folded piece of paper. "Iggy did it during lunch," he whispered.

I opened it up and saw a drawing of two bowling alleys side by side, each complete with the ball-return chute and ten pins. Then I noticed the tiny line that ran along the front of the alley closest to the stage, wrapped around the front corner, went back along the right side, and rose into the air. The end was connected to a lumpy bag.

It was neatly labeled, too, with arrows pointing to certain items — SCREW EYE HOOKS, FISHING LINE, STAGE-RIGGING CORDS, FLOUR SACK — all written in Iggy's very neat, very precise scientific hand. The one I liked best was at the end of an arrow pointing to a spot on the foul line where a bowler would release the ball: TRIPWIRE.

"So it's going to happen?" I asked in a thin whisper.

"*Alea iacta est,*" Philip replied just as quietly but with a certain fierceness. His eyes were very big and hard-looking.

I looked at Vero, and he shrugged, raising his hands palms up in a way that suggested he had no idea what Philip just said, but he agreed with him completely. Then Vero smiled and added quietly, "She's toast."

16

Tick. Tick. Tick. Tick.

IT TOOK A FEW DAYS for Mayor to work his executive magic, but eventually he was able to persuade Bernie to let him and some of the other guys help. "I told him my mother made me volunteer. You know, as an act of charity," Mayor said. "Bernie said I'd get into heaven with such good deeds."

Without knowing it, Bernie helped move the Plan forward. There were two small rooms just outside the stage-level doors to the auditorium. Mrs. Ryan taught one of the third-grade classes in the room on the left. The one on the right was empty except for a few desks and twenty years of dust.

Bernie had Mayor, Iggy, Vero, and Tom-Tom haul some boxes into the empty room. Then he didn't so much dawdle as dither. He suddenly remembered that Sister Rose Mary had mentioned that they might need the room for another class in the fall, and he went off upstairs to see if there might be another room or a big closet where stuff could be left, so he wouldn't have to move it all again later. This gave Iggy lots of time to study the bowling lanes and refine the Plan.

"There are no free rides in this world," my mom said whenever I asked for something that wasn't absolutely necessary. Which was most of the things I wanted. This also meant that I couldn't, say, just get on a bus and not pay the fare. If I was going for a ride, I had to have money. Now Mayor and Iggy informed me that I had to pay the fare for this ride.

"If we're going ahead with this, we'll need money," Mayor said. He was in his organizational mode. "We have to lay in supplies." Three five-pound bags of flour, one hundred feet of ten-pound fishing line, eye hooks, and a can of flat black paint.

"For starters," Iggy added. He warned me that there might be more expenses as the Plan evolved and was perfected. For instance, the cords that held up the scenery were just in front of the bowling alleys, so he'd have to devise a way to hang a cord over the middle of an alley. And this might require more hardware.

"Do we really need three bags of flour?"

"We have to test this out in Vero's garage first."

Mayor was trying to be patient with me. "Probably a couple of times at least. We only get one shot at her, and we want this to work perfectly, don't we?"

The "we" was interesting. It was clear that "we" were all in this together, but I was expected to pay for it. I was about to ask how much money the others would be chipping in, when I remembered that Philip's father had lost his job around the same time as Erin's (Margaret's) father had. So it didn't seem fair to want money from him. Instead, I asked how much might be needed to start, and Mayor told me. It was, like, a year's worth of salty potato sticks! I must have groaned as I dug into my pocket for the small wad of dollar bills Dad had paid me for ripping up and bagging the kitchen tiles. This revenge stuff was expensive.

Later in the afternoon I felt a lot different about paying the money. Sister Angelica suddenly told us to take out a piece of paper. This usually meant a quiz, so there was a lot of moaning and grumbling. "No quiz today," she told us. "I want you to write a brief thank-you letter. Remember to set it up like the example on page seventy-six of the *Language Arts* book. You can use your book, but I want the text to be your own."

I opened the book and checked out the sample

letter, which was very neat-looking. The writer was thanking his grandmother for the new tie she gave him for his birthday. A tie for a present is not cause for thanks in my book, but I guess you have to give grandmothers a break on this sort of thing. What was I supposed to write about?

Not to thank someone for coming to my birthday party or even for a gift (birthday, Christmas, or whenever). I wanted to stay clear of anything that hinted that I'd cribbed from the letter in the *Language Arts* book. And no mention of grandmas, or even grandpas, I assumed. I could thank Mom and Dad for putting up with me, which seemed original but also odd. I mean, don't all parents put up with their annoying kids (besides the really good-smart kids who never seem to do anything wrong)? I wasn't sure what to do, but time was running out, so I wrote the date at the top of the page. The correct date this time, as ordered.

I stared at the paper.

Then inspiration struck. I'm not saying it was genius, but it was unusual, especially coming from a boy. Unusual in a good way, I hoped.

I wrote my name and address at the top in the center, as page 76 showed. Then I wrote Kathy Gathers's name and address below that on the left.

"Dear Kathy," I began. "I want to thank you for inviting me to your pajama party last Friday night." There was more, and I worked really hard not to say anything even remotely bad about Kathy or her party. The party was great, according to my thank-you letter, which included a compliment about her pink teddy bear PJs.

Yes, I know, I said I wouldn't write any more stories about Kathy, but this wasn't really a story. It was a letter about a party. So, technically, I wasn't breaking my promise. I was probably "skating on thin ice," as Mom always said when I was being annoying, but I knew that and, as Mayor might have advised, planned accordingly. I didn't tell any of my friends what my letter was about, because they might spread the word around the class and make it a bigger deal than it was.

This particular plan worked until Sister Angelica studied our letters and called us up one by one to talk about them. When I got to her desk, she was holding my letter in both hands, head bent over, reading it very, very carefully. She looked up at me. "Did this actually happen?" she asked in a quiet but demanding voice.

"Well, Sister," I began, then paused a beat or two to consider my answer. "I think she had a" — I didn't want to say "pajama party" out loud because there were a lot of kids milling around. I pointed to my letter—"one a few weeks ago." Another pause to consider what to say next, and then I rushed to add, "But I wasn't invited or anything. That would be too, you know, weird and all"—my voice became so soft it was hard even for me to hear what I was saying—"for a boy, um, to be there."

"I'm glad you realize that," she mumbled. She put my letter flat on her desk and pointed to a sentence. "It needs a comma here," she said. She took up her red ballpoint pen, clicked it so the point appeared, and inserted the comma. Then she circled it and said, "You need to rewrite the entire letter." She handed me my letter, implying that I had been dismissed.

She told me that when I was finished, I should come up and stand in line (quietly) while she went through other people's letters. So I went back to my desk and wrote a new letter, adding the comma. I was back at her desk five minutes later. No one was in front of me, so she looked at my letter right away, scowled, then took her red pen and added another comma in another sentence, circling it as before. "You need to correct all the punctuation in the letter," she said, accenting the word "all" and giving her head a little shake. "Please redo it again correctly."

I went back to my desk, wondering why she couldn't have pointed out this additional comma earlier to save me some time. I rewrote the letter, adding the comma. I might have mumbled something under my breath, because Vero asked what was the matter. I told him about the commas, and he mumbled something. Mumbled togetherness felt nice right then, I have to tell you. "Let me see that," he ordered, taking my letter. He studied my paper and began to chuckle. "Did you really go to her pajama party? Sounds like fun." After I told him I'd made up the whole thing, he pointed out a couple of other punctuation errors. He handed it back to me. "There. That should shut her up!"

I fixed the punctuation, then went up to show Sister Angelica. There were two kids in front of me.

Here is where it all turned really sour. I mean, having to rewrite a silly thank-you letter again and again was bad enough. Now it got *bad*—with exclamation points!!!!!

Mary Claire Danes was at the front of the line. She handed her letter to Sister Angelica, who took it and looked it over. "See here, Mary Claire." Sister Angelica pointed to the paper and said, "It needs a comma there. Go back and put it in, and you'll be finished."

What?! She leaves a comma out and gets to stick it in and DOESN'T HAVE TO REWRITE THE ENTIRE LETTER? I knew my brain was screaming too loud, but this wasn't right. Mary Claire was one of the good-smart kids (and I clearly wasn't), but shouldn't justice be meted out evenly? (That last part was something I heard Uncle Arthur say once or twice, though I can't remember why he said it. But it did sound right.)

Joey Spano was next. He showed his paper to Angelica.

"You have very nice handwriting, Joey. Beautiful, really. There are two words spelled incorrectly" — she pointed to the paper — "cross them out and write in the correct spelling just above. You can use the spelling book to check them."

Joey was not what I'd ever call a good or a smart kid (though he was better than I was in both categories). He was a perfectly nice kid who also happened to be wide enough to help me hide from Sister Angelica. It was obvious that Angelica had targeted me for special treatment.

I gave her my paper and waited for the guillotine blade to fall. Because I knew it would. And she didn't disappoint.

"The punctuation is fine," she said coolly—not, I noticed, ever using my first name as she'd done with Mary Claire and Joey. "But . . ."

Yes, there was a "but." I'd spelled a word incorrectly, and the red pen did its thing on my paper. I was sick of rewriting this dumb letter and actually wished Sister Angelica would just stab me in my left arm with her red ballpoint pen and get it over with.

Back at my desk, I was able to get Vero, Mayor, and Iggy involved in finding all the misspelled words. Sister Angelica was busy looking at other kids' papers, so we were able to pass my letter back and forth without much trouble. All of them, by the way, liked the letter and thought it was very unusual, not at all insulting to Kathy Gathers.

I was back at Sister Angelica's desk a few minutes later, waiting for the verdict. "The punctuation and spelling are fine," Sister Angelica said. I felt my shoulders and back relax just a little. I was seconds away from being free of this torture. "But this didn't really happen, did it? This party."

"No, Sister."

She pointed to Kathy's name. "Then I think you should change the name and address."

"Yes, Sister." By that I meant I would never use a real kid's name in any future assignment, letter, or story, but that wasn't what *she* meant.

"Good. Rewrite it with a different name and address and you'll be finished."

"Yes, Sister," I said very quietly through clenched teeth.

By the time I got back to my desk, my head was throbbing, my thoughts were white-hot and madly, blindingly flashing. This is not fair, I told myself. Not that I needed telling. I could feel the second hand of the clock in Sister Rose Mary's office moving forward a click at a time. Tick. Tick. Tick. Tick. This. Is. Not. Fair. This. Is. Not. Fair. I thought my head might explode at any tick. I glared at Sister Angelica and wanted to scream, *If it's a war you want, Sister, you've got it.*

17

My Fat Duck Hop-Waddle Jig

MY ANGER WAS like a roller-coaster ride. I know that doesn't sound very smart, but after all, I was only a sixth grader. Most of the time I wasn't very angry, just always simmering annoyed. But then I'd feel the anger building a little at a time. Like a roller-coaster car slowly going up a steep hill. Clack, clack, clack. Then something would push me over the top — like writing a stupid, stupid . . . did I mention stupid? . . . thank-you letter a thousand, million times! — and it would all go downhill from there, without brakes, to crash at the bottom and explode into pieces while every rider with me was screaming.

I went back to my desk. My anger must have been showing on my face. Vero leaned over and whispered, "What's the matter?"

I murmured, "Everything." Though I think I said another word before "everything."

I redid my letter. Since this was war, I decided I had to make it almost the same, though different enough so *she* couldn't complain. I addressed my letter to Ken Gabler and wrote the *K* and the *G* extra big so *she* couldn't miss it. I thanked Ken for the great pajama party and changed the pink teddy bear PJs to Pittsburgh Pirates PJs. Still, I felt a little victorious when *she* grudgingly said it was okay. But clearly, *she* didn't love my letter. *She* gave me a crummy 73 percent.

I was still so angry when school was out that I stalked away from my friends, didn't buy any salty potato sticks, and even walked on the opposite side of Kearny Avenue so I wouldn't meet the three high school girls in their short plaid skirts and tight sweaters. They spotted me, though, and Mr. MacGullion's daughter yelled across the street, "Hey, Jim Murphy Jr. How're you doing?" I'd been seen, and I didn't want to seem rude, so I waved and said "Hi," but even this little encounter was ruined by what Sister Angelica Rose had done.

Dad came home early and made bacon-wrapped

hot dogs with melted cheese. Plus Boston baked beans with a lot of bacon in them. Usually anything with bacon put me in a good mood, but not that night. After I grunted some answers to the standard "how was your day" questions, Mom said, "You seem a bit peckish tonight, Jimmy. Any reason?"

I muttered "No" quietly, but by then Dad had said, "He's hardly touched his dinner. I'm not sure he's peckish."

My brother laughed and added, "Peckish, shmeckish, wreckage," and laughed some more.

"What does peckish have to do with his dinner?" Mom asked.

"Peckish means hungry," Dad explained.

"Peckish means grumpy," Mom countered. She seemed pretty sure about the definition.

"When I'm hungry," Jerry said, "I'm usually grumpy, too."

"Hungry," Dad said to Mom. "Grumpy isn't a primary definition. But we can look it up after dinner."

"If he ate his hot dog in one angry gulp," Jerry offered, "he could be peckish in every way possible."

Usually this kind of odd circular conversation was a distraction and sort of fun, but it just made me even more annoyed. Or should I say more peckish? I even grunted my answers when Ellen called, which didn't make me feel any better, in case you're wondering.

I was so out of sorts at school the next day that I didn't pay any attention to what Sister Angelica was trying to teach us. Why bother, I figured, when I'm destined to be criticized, get low grades, and have additional comments added to my red MURPHY folder. Then things got even worse.

Yes, worse.

It was Thursday, so that afternoon my second-grade escort arrived to take me to the banana rehearsal. There were some chuckles from a few kids in my class (Roger seemed particularly pleased at what I was going through), but when I stood up, Sister Angelica gave me a hard, nasty look that suggested I was disrupting her class of good-smart kids. I couldn't figure out why she was scowling at me, though I did wonder if they had run out of cherry Jell-O on Wednesday night before she got any. What I did know was that her being angry wasn't fair. I didn't actually volunteer to be the Green Banana, now, did I?

When I got to the auditorium, I found that all the Yellow Bananas were in costume. Here's the thing. Sister Mary Brian had mentioned costumes during other rehearsals, but for some reason I thought the Yellow Bananas would be wearing yellow rain slickers with those silly, floppy yellow rain hats. Every kid had one, even me. But here they all were in real banana costumes. I shivered at what might follow.

Sister Mary Brian was fussing with some kid's costume, making sure that it fit and the kid could breathe. She was having trouble getting some of the bigger kids into their banana peels, and she seemed distracted and frustrated. Besides, a bunch of kids had discovered that if they lowered their banana heads, they could have a banana-head duel, while others danced around and bumped into each other like bumper cars at an amusement park. "Children," she said impatiently, "please settle down while I get Charles here into his costume." She noticed me and pointed stage right. "James, your costume is over there. Could you climb into it so we can get started?"

My spine went numb when I saw my costume. It was gigantic. Sister Rose Vincent gigantic, maybe seven feet tall. There was a huge zipper down the back. The inside of the costume looked like the interior of a zeppelin, with all sorts of wooden braces, struts, and cross frames, plus a padded harness to hold it upright on my shoulders. And it was heavy. I could barely lift it. The Yellow Banana costumes looked very light. You don't have banana-head duels in a heavy costume.

I must have seemed confused, so Sister Mary Brian called over to me, "Mr. Danes said you should wear it the way you wear football shoulder pads." She finally got Charles into his yellow banana and zipped him up. "Children, please. We need to practice with our costumes on so we can do our dance. The first show is in three weeks. And don't run into each other or the costumes might break." I was still looking into my costume and wishing I could disappear. "James, just climb in, put your feet through the holes at the bottom, put your arms out the side holes, and slide the harness over your shoulders."

She really didn't have to tell me how to put it on. Just looking at it made it obvious what I had to do. But thinking about getting into it told me something else. Once I was in, I would have—I'm not sure how to say this without committing some sort of major sin— I would have a large part of the green banana sticking out between my legs. I gave Sister Mary Brian a pleading look, which she ignored. "James, just get inside so I can zip you up. We've already wasted a lot of time."

I put it on as directed. The leg holes were so tight that my pants rolled up inside. Once I had the harness over my shoulders, I heard the big zipper locking me in. "Okay," she said with a weary cheerfulness. "Everyone into our Victory-V, and we'll begin."

I discovered a number of things about my costume as Sister Mary Brian hurried to the piano. The inside smelled like pine wood, glue, and paint because the thick green paint covering the outside had seeped through the fabric. It was also hard to see much through the little porthole opening where my eyes were, so I had to lean forward to locate the front of the Victory-V. Mr. Danes (Mary Claire's father) was an engineer of some sort, and he had built wooden frames that met at each end but widened out in the middle, just like the peel sections of a banana. This meant that my (now bare) legs were not able to come together. Walking meant waddling like a fat duck. Despite all obstacles, I managed to hop-waddle to my spot.

Sister Mary Brian ordered us to stand up tall, keep our heads up, and face forward. She had several Yellow Bananas take a step to the right or the left to straighten the line. Then she called out, "And one . . . and two . . . and three!"

The piano thumped into action, and so did I. What happened next is hard to describe because it began and ended so quickly. I step-hopped forward with my left foot, swung my right foot to touch my left foot, kicked myself in the knee instead, and started spinning like a top on the toes of my left foot. I waved my arms this way and that to stay balanced, but after three spins I fell over backwards onto the stage floor. And continued to rotate. Like one of those arcade games where the guy gives the wheel a spin and shouts, "Around and around she goes, where she stops nobody knows." Only I wasn't a "she" Green Banana.

From behind I heard small voices squeak, "Sister, Sister, the Green Banana fell down!" Sister Mary Brian was focused on playing the piano (with gusto) and hadn't noticed that I'd gone over. When she finally did, I heard the loudest-ever, frustrated, discordant bang of ten notes on the keyboard.

I was still going round and round, but slowing down, when I heard the thud of her sensible shoes hurrying up onto the stage. Finally I came to a stop, my head pointing toward the front of the stage.

"What's going on here?"

I was staring straight up and feeling very helpless and a little nauseated. A turtle on its back probably feels the same way. Then Sister Mary Brian's face came into view, but because she was standing at the top of the costume, her white-coifed face was upside down.

"I didn't fall on purpose," I managed to gasp. I was becoming aware that there wasn't much air inside the costume, and it was hot as well. I guess the thick green paint had made my banana airtight.

"Are you okay?" she asked.

"Yes, Sister," I answered. Of course I would have said that even if I'd broken my leg.

"Okay, everyone. We need to spin James around so he's facing forward and help him to his feet." Which happened a second later, but I swear Al asked if they could spin me around a few more times because it looked like fun. I was happy that Sister Mary Brian said no.

We rehearsed for almost an hour straight. I couldn't get my sneakers to touch the way they were supposed to. Sister Mary Brian told me to just slide my feet as close as possible to the correct position and keep moving. To stay balanced and upright, I had to wave my arms around a little. Instead of a nicely executed box step, I was doing a wild sort of feet-flying, arms-waving jig. Sister Mary Brian seemed happy enough and even told the Yellow Bananas that they could imitate me. As long as they kept to the beat.

When I was finally released and stepped out of my Green Banana costume, I was drenched in sweat, tired, and about as happy as a rattlesnake that's been stepped on. I even thought about offering more cash so Iggy could figure out how to get Al the Second Grader's punji sticks to work. It was war, and — as the saying goes — all's fair in love and war.

I knew the punji sticks wouldn't happen, but thinking about them made me feel a little better. I wanted to push the Plan forward in any way possible, no matter how much of my tile-removal money it would cost.

I was about to leave when Sister Mary Brian made an announcement. "The show for your parents and relatives will be on the Monday before Thanksgiving," she told us. "We'll do a full rehearsal program for the entire school the week before, to work out any kinks."

What? I had figured a show for these kids' parents and relatives wouldn't be so bad, because I would be in my costume and no one would know who I was. But a show for the entire school . . . It wouldn't take long for everybody to realize I was the one doing the Fat Duck Hop-Waddle Jig. And that included Kathy Gathers.

18

SHE HAS TO BE STOPPED!!!!

IF THIS WERE a movie, loud, insistent music with a throbbing bass beat would start playing now. On the screen would be speeded-up action scenes of things getting done in a flash to let viewers know that time was marching along quickly, but they shouldn't worry, the bad guys would be taken care of soon.

Unfortunately, the story you are reading is true. Nothing hurried along. And the only music I heard in my head was banana related.

The guys had helped Bernie clear more stuff from the stage (it's amazing how much can accumulate over two or three decades). Iggy had been able to study the setup and work out some details of the device, which, naturally, would cost more than I had anticipated. To run the scenery cord over the alley, he needed two large eyebolts to screw into a wooden beam. That might cost a few dollars, but since he hadn't figured out the tripwire mechanism, he said there would probably be more expenses. Even so, he decided that we should test the bags to see how they worked. We did this one Saturday in Vero's garage, which was pretty big and had a tall roof.

Iggy wanted to check the arc of the swing to make sure the bag would hit someone Sister Angelica's height square in the chest. Squints climbed up into the rafters, and on Iggy's signal he swung the bag filled with flour . . . and the ten-pound test line broke. So we (I) had to buy twenty-pound test line. Vero volunteered to take the first actual hit to see how the bag exploded. But it didn't explode at all. It whomped Vero in the chest so hard that he flew out of the garage and ended up on his back in the driveway.

"Back to the drawing board," Mayor said matter-of-factly.

"I'm not paying for a drawing board," I blurted out. Which earned me a look from Mayor that suggested I should study the chapter titled "Common English Phrases and Their Origins and Meanings" in the red *Language Arts* book.

Iggy went home and thought about how to get the bag to explode in a shower of flour; Vero went hunting for the mannequin his grandmother used when sewing dresses. The bruise on his chest had convinced him that a nonhuman test target was the safest way to go. A week later, Iggy said he'd figured out the exploding bag, which required a helium-filled balloon inside each bag and five test explosions to prove it worked, plus five more five-pound sacks of flour. Can we guess who paid for this?

Then Bernie gave us our deadline. Seems that one afternoon while the guys were helping Bernie, he happened to mention that Sister Angelica was going to announce the formation of a girls' bowling team at the rehearsal performance of the show. She'd told him she was hoping to throw a couple of balls to demonstrate the redone lanes. Every kid in the school would be there, so this would be a good way to ensure that a lot of girls heard about the bowling team.

This development was good for another reason. I knew I was going to be embarrassed publicly during the rehearsal, when my classmates and everyone in school would see me as the Green Banana, but now —if the details could be worked out— Sister Angelica would be embarrassed too. Bigtime.

October and Halloween came and went, the leaves started to change colors and drop, November began, and the days got colder. During all this time, progress was being made on rigging the exploding flour ball. While Bernie was scouting for additional places upstairs to store things, Iggy was able to put in the black-painted eye hooks and measure how long the fishing line would have to be. Iggy wanted the line cut and painted black in advance to save time when he installed it. It took some doing, but he even got the big eyebolt in before Bernie got back. He also had three balloons inflated and the flour balls assembled and ready to be deployed. He hadn't figured out how to trigger the device, but he said he was thinking over a solution, so we shouldn't worry. Oh, and we wouldn't be able to test a balloon, as Vero's grandfather was pressing grapes in the garage to make wine. It was all beginning to feel like a scene from one of Al the Second Grader's comic books, where a lot is happening but the outcome is still in doubt.

As all of this was moving forward, my anger began to cool, and I was on that slow clack-clack-clack climb back up the roller coaster. I wanted the "job" done, but I wasn't frothing at the mouth anymore, if you know what I mean. In fact, I spent more time adding up what I'd spent on revenge than actually anticipating it. I'd finished taking up all the tiles and bagging them, and Dad told me he'd show me how to prepare the wood floor and lay the new tiles down — and he would pay me for that, too! Which was great and also annoying, since as fast as my money came in, it went out for "tactical expenses," as Mayor explained in his executive voice. Then Sister Angelica managed to reignite my anger.

One afternoon she suddenly stood up and said, "Everyone take out your *Language Arts* book. We're on page forty-three." This was mostly a spelling book, but for some reason whoever wrote it thought their title sounded better. More official or impressive or something. Usually Sister Angelica would read out the week's spelling words, so we'd know how to say them, and then explain what they meant. Today she looked to the back row and added, "Philip, would you please say the extra-credit spelling words for the class?"

Philip looked startled and trapped, but he stood up with his red *Language Arts* book and thumbed to page 43. I could see that he was worried, not to mention dazed and confused, and his face was already beginning to redden. He hemmed and hawed a few times, then coughed to clear his throat.

The regular spelling words were hard enough to say, but the extra-credit words were especially tongue twisting. Philip studied the list for a second, then paused and looked at Angelica. Everyone in class glanced at the list of extra-credit words, so we all knew the first one was "epiphany." Angelica nodded for him to begin.

"E . . . e . . . e . . . p . . . p . . . piss . . ."

So right away there was a good deal of laughing. I might have smiled myself. I mean, come on, it was funny. Then I noticed that Philip's cheeks and the tips of his ears had turned neon red.

Sister Angelica shushed the class and then said to Philip, "It's eh-*pif*-ah-nee. Let's say it together."

The together idea really didn't work, since she barreled ahead and said, "Eh-*pif*-ah-nee," but Philip only said, "Eh . . . eh . . . eh . . ." And not much more before some kids began giggling. I'm sure I heard Roger's whiny little voice in there. I didn't mind him bullying me, but mocking Philip was way too much.

Angelica drifted down the aisle toward us. Not that I was doing anything. I wanted to say something to defend Philip, to stop Angelica, but I also didn't want to make things worse for him. Or me. She stopped a few feet from me and told Philip they would try it again. "Eh," she said, and Philip echoed with a feeble "eh." "Pif" came next, and Philip said, "P . . . p . . . pif."

Some kids repeated Philip's "p . . . p . . . pif," but Angelica quieted the room with a menacing look. I wanted Uncle Arthur there to shout *I object!*—that's how angry I was getting. Clack, clack, clack. But all I did was raise my hand a little and mumble, "Ah, Sister . . ."

I wanted to say, as nicely as I could, that putting Philip on exhibition like this wasn't right. I figured that she got angry at me for pointing out that Sister Jane was missing a finger, so why shouldn't she be embarrassed for embarrassing Philip? Right?

She was a few feet away from the desk, and I know she heard what I said. Without even looking at me, she put her hand up like a traffic cop to keep me quiet.

Angelica lowered her hand slowly. She and Philip tried to say the word again, and failed. And even though fewer kids laughed, my brain started to sizzle, and I knew I was on the verge of something, though exactly what wasn't clear, and that scared me a little.

She turned back to Philip and smiled. "We should try it again, Philip. Practice makes perfect."

She said the word; then Philip said, "Eh . . . *pif* . . . *pif* . . . a . . ." He stopped, took a breath.

At which point Vero said to him, loud enough for

everyone to hear, *"Non c'è nulla da temere quando gli amici sono vicino."* Vero's grandparents lived with his parents and pretty much spoke nothing but Italian, and they and his parents often had long conversations in that language. Vero told me he started to learn Italian so they couldn't talk about him behind his back.

Philip looked at him, gave a quick smile. I knew that Philip studied all sorts of language books, but I was a little surprised when he answered Vero with, *"Ringrazio, il mio buon amico. Ti ringrazio."*

Angelica had stopped cold in the aisle and glared at both Vero and Philip with a terrible, dark look on her face. Vero had crossed his arms over his chest, completely ignoring her wrath. He was feeling the same as I was, and he wasn't going to back down or even tell Angelica what he'd said. Philip turned back to Angelica. His cheeks and ears seemed a little less red.

Sister Angelica took a menacing step toward them. She was about to say something when I opened my mouth and blurted out very loudly, *"J'accuse* you!"

Both Vero and Philip wheeled around to give me a questioning look. My outburst made no sense whatsoever. It wasn't Italian, for one thing; it was French. A bit of dialogue I remembered from a Three Musketeers movie that meant "I accuse." I didn't know how to say "I accuse you" all in French, so I tacked on the English "you." But it had exactly the effect I'd hoped for.

Angelica turned on me and said very sharply, "You, Master Murphy, will keep perfectly quiet, and you will see me after class. Do you understand?"

I said "Sure" in a deliberately sulky and defiant voice and faced forward. My eyes bored into Joey Spano's ample back as I fought to avoid a panic attack.

I steeled myself for the worst, but nothing happened. I heard Sister Angelica take in several gulps of air. Then she addressed Philip in a fake-calm voice. "Let's try this again, shall we, Philip? I'll say the word and you repeat it."

Philip didn't have much choice, but he seemed okay with moving forward and getting it all over with.

And so it went, Angelica saying the word syllable by syllable and Philip repeating it. Then they went on to the second word, which happened to be "serendipity." If you thought "epiphany" was a struggle for Philip, you should have heard "serendipity" being pronounced. And there were three more extra-credit words!

Eventually and thankfully, it ended, and Philip

—looking tired and absolutely drained—was allowed to sit down and disappear while Angelica went to the front of the class. She had completely ignored Vero, and I was glad about that. I had learned over the years that bullies like to pick on one person at a time, usually the weakest, and I guess it was my time. I was still fuming, and all I could think to do was scribble a note to Iggy that said "SHE HAS TO BE STOPPED!!!!"

19

On the Seesaw

HERE'S A SHORTENED VERSION of how my after-school meeting went. I appeared at Sister Angelica's desk as ordered, and she gave me a hard, tough look. I just stared back and made believe I was completely innocent.

"How dare you challenge me in my classroom?"

"You were embarrassing my friend," I said as quietly and in as assured a way as I could. But I was shaking a little, too, since I'd never spoken to an adult like this before, let alone a nun. "He stammers when he talks English."

"I know. I'm trying to help him," she replied.

"By making him stammer?" Now, this was absolutely the best (and only) decent one-liner I had ever delivered in school, and no other kid was there to hear it.

She was obviously frustrated and annoyed. Clearly she was talking to an idiot (me), and I would never understand why she did what she did, no matter how carefully she explained it. Instead, she told me to sit down and write "I will not interrupt in class" one hundred times. Which I did quickly. The sentence fit easily onto one line of the paper, so I numbered every line and wrote "I" all the way to the bottom, then went back and did the same with "will" and all the other words — the Henry Ford mass-production assembly-line approach to punishment sentences.

Three pages of this, and I was done. She did take a parting shot, of course. Not a slap-in-the-head kind of shot, the nun kind. "And if you ever, *ever*" — she paused here, then added in a deliberately controlled voice — "do anything of that sort again . . ."

There was more, but I felt myself getting unpleasantly and dangerously lightheaded — dangerous because I didn't know how bad the lightheadedness would get or what I might do. I decided to tune her out before I said something that would get me additional punishment. I was alert enough to realize when I should say "Yes, Sister," at which point she dismissed me with a wave of her hand.

I had a bad night, mostly wondering what Angelica

would do to me the next day. I had, after all, brought all the attention to myself and managed to do my hundred sentences pretty easily, too easily, so why wouldn't she be plotting some sort of evil revenge? The good news was that Al the Second Grader had saved the day. He heard that Iggy had everything pretty much figured out — the placement of the eye hooks, hooking up the fishing line, the helium-balloon-filled sacks of flour — but wasn't sure how it would all be triggered. Al the Second Grader, like an ever-resourceful Cub Scout, dug back through his comic book collection and appeared with a possible answer.

He brought in a comic called *The World at War in the Pacific*. About fighting on tropical islands during World War II. I didn't know anything else about it, since I saw only one page, which had several panels of drawings that showed how a clever GI rigged up a booby trap to "neutralize" enemy soldiers. One had a clear drawing of how the device was triggered.

Iggy looked at the comic, grabbed it more dramatically than he'd ever done anything else, and said, "I can work with that!" His eyes narrowed as he studied every little detail of the drawing.

"Can we put the punji sticks back in?" Al the Second Grader asked eagerly.

"Not possible," Iggy muttered, still eyeballing the drawing in the comic book.

"Can't we use Super Glue or something like that?" You had to hand it to Al. He was deranged, helpful, *and* persistent. You never know — if he ever developed a sense of humor, he might become president of the United States someday.

"What Iggy means," Mayor pointed out quickly and calmly, "is that there's not enough time to work out all the details and test it."

"I could find some other comics that show . . ."

"Hey, kid," Squints grumbled ominously. He took off his big black glasses and glared at Al. "No means *no*, okay? So shut up already. Jeez, why are we still talking to a second grader anyway?"

Tom-Tom leaned toward Al, nodding in agreement. "Sometimes," he said, "the best results aren't the most obvious."

"But this is a big help, Al." Mayor pointed to the comic book in Iggy's hands. "So thanks."

Nothing much happened in class that day or the next. Angelica seemed very tense, and I know I was. I had a feeling she was just waiting for a chance to strike, so I spent most of my time hiding behind Joey Spano and telling myself not to say anything that might get me buried. And daydreaming of absolute revenge.

The daydream went like this. Angelica shows everyone in the auditorium that the alleys are ready to be used. She slides up to the foul line, her sensible shoe hits the tripwire, and down swings the flour bag in a perfect arc. Bam, she gets nailed, and flour dust flies everywhere.

Of course the auditorium goes wild, some cheering, everybody laughing hysterically. Nuns are running every which way, trying to restore order and help the thoroughly dusted Sister Angelica. And then there's the hunt for me.

This is where my brain took a perfect daydream and ruined it with reality. You see, I'm in the audience with everybody else and enjoying the show, but when I hear the familiar *Where is Master Murphy?* I freeze and look around. And see that Kathy Gathers is shocked and horrified by what has just happened and is staring at me. Not a loving stare, by the way.

I started wondering if maybe the exploding flour bag might not be the best way to impress Kathy. I even wondered if I should call it off.

But giving up on it wasn't really an option. Mayor, Iggy, Vero, Squints, Tom-Tom, and Philip had put in a lot of time, and I didn't want to disappoint them. And think what horrible things Al the Second Grader might cook up to murderlate me for this betrayal! Because that's what I felt it would be. And then there was Philip. We were doing all this because Angelica seemed to go out of her way to embarrass me *and* Philip, so I wasn't sure I had the right to cancel it on my own.

It took a few days, but eventually Iggy said he thought he'd figured out how to take the comic book drawing and make it actually work. Seems the comic book artist had an imagination, especially when it came to blowing stuff up, but not a lot of actual mechanical skill.

I remember hearing Iggy announcing this success and feeling relieved. This whole revenge thing had stretched from day one of school into November, and I wanted it over with. Plus it was constantly eating up money (mine!). Yes, the trigger device needed several pieces of hardware.

So on we went, day after day, until the Monday in the second week of November, when two developments came to my attention. Before school, Mayor told me that he and his crew would install the exploding flour ball, fishing line, and trigger device at noon.

Then later that day a message arrived from Sister Mary Brian saying the trial performance of the entire show would happen on Wednesday afternoon. A little sooner than expected.

Next, Bernie threw a wrench into the works (that "threw a wrench into the works" is a phrase I spotted in "Common English Phrases and Their Origins and Meanings," in the *Language Arts* book, in case you're wondering where it came from). Anyway, he came down to the auditorium on Monday to discover a bunch of first graders sliding on his newly finished, very shiny bowling alleys, scuffing them with their black rubber-soled shoes. He got them off and immediately declared an emergency. When Mayor and the guys showed up later to get the stage cleared and make sure the curtain worked, Bernie was on his hands and knees buffing out the black marks on the alleys and muttering darkly.

"Some of you boys can move those boxes up to the first-floor storage area. I'll need one of you"—he pointed to Mayor—"to help me rope off the alleys so these little hooligans don't mark them up any more before Wednesday." He glared sharply at the little kids who were standing innocently to the side, waiting to rehearse.

While the others wrestled boxes up the stairs, Mayor set up four wooden posts (which were really the ends of a stage prop fence), one at every corner of the alleys. Bernie took a long spool of yellow plastic police ribbon that repeated the words CRIME SCENE —DO NOT CROSS over and over, and he and Mayor tied the ribbon to the posts. The good news, Mayor reported later, was that Bernie was still annoyed with the little kids and was constantly scowling at them, so he hadn't noticed the eye hooks. The bad news was that Bernie hung around the stage to protect his alleys, so the fishing line, exploding ball, and triggering device couldn't be attached and armed (that's the word Iggy used).

When I heard that the device hadn't been rigged, I must have looked stunned. Mayor worked hard to keep me calm. "Iggy thinks it's still doable. Right, Iggy?"

"Absolutely. The eye hooks are in, and the ceiling cord is the perfect length and in perfect position. The fishing line is cut to the exact size and painted and ready to go." He shrugged. "All I have to do is get the fishing line tied to the first eye hook and threaded through the rest of the eye hooks, and get the scenery cord over the alley with the ball attached." It all sounded like an overwhelming amount of work to me, but Iggy said confidently, "Maybe tomorrow — we'll see."

Unfortunately, the daydream kept reappearing to haunt me, especially the Kathy Gathers part. What would happen if I was eventually connected to the prank? Not good. What would happen to me? Probably painfully not good. And how would my parents take it? Especially not good. And what would Kathy Gathers think of me? Really, really not good at all.

After thinking this over (and over and over), I understood that it all came down to which was more important: getting revenge or still having a chance with Kathy. I felt like I was on a giant seesaw — one second, revenge was what I wanted, the next it was not to make Kathy think I was even more of a loser than she already did. Up, down, up, down . . .

On Tuesday, Mayor reported that they had managed to sneak two balls into the auditorium (the second in case the first one suddenly deflated) and got one attached to the cord. Iggy was able to tie fishing line to one eye hook and thread it through the others, but Bernie came back and hovered around again, so he couldn't rig up the triggering device. And Iggy still wasn't one hundred percent sure it would work. When I asked for the odds on it working, he said fifty-fifty. Anyway, the final hookup would have to wait until Wednesday — the day of the big rehearsal.

20
JUMP!!!!

ON WEDNESDAY just before noon, Sister Angelica told Mayor, Iggy, Squints, Philip, and Tom-Tom that they should go directly to the auditorium to help Bernie and have lunch later. I was left on my own to stew and wonder what was happening.

I got to the cafeteria, took a tray, and slid it along the rails without taking anything. I was too nervous to eat. My cousin Sophia offered me a new menu item that looked strangely lime green and lumpy, and I passed on it as politely as possible. Then I noticed that Sister Rose Vincent wasn't guarding the door.

I wanted to know what was going on with the exploding flour ball, and I was feeling the seesaw tilting toward requesting a delay. This was my "better safe than sorry" position. Since I wasn't sure what would happen afterward (especially with Kathy) if it worked,

I took a weaselly approach. I even came up with a way to convince the guys: we would delay so we could have time to plan what to do post-revenge. With Rose Vincent gone, now was my chance to slip out and get to the auditorium. I put my tray back and walked out the door as if I were on some very important mission. Head up, a slight *I'm not up to anything* smile on my face in case one of the nuns on aisle patrol spotted me.

There were several routes to choose from. I decided to go the most direct way, across the small outdoor courtyard that connects the new and old schools. I could zip down to the auditorium, talk the guys into a slight delay, and zip back up in just a minute or two. So out I went.

As the landing door clicked closed behind me, I started to walk slowly across the courtyard. It couldn't have been any more than seventy-five feet to the door I was heading toward. It was probably locked, but kids often went up and down the steps to go to the bathroom, and I hoped to get one of them to push it open for me. I was halfway there when I heard the basement door to the convent squeak open.

A moment of panic followed, and then my brain screamed *HIDE!* Luckily, this was where the few sad-looking green plants at St. Stephen's existed — two anemic pine trees and some scraggly sticker bushes. I squeezed past a sticker bush that was as friendly as Al's punji sticks and ducked behind one of the trees. Whoever had come out of the convent would probably disappear inside the school in a matter of seconds.

I was standing there waiting for the person's exit when I heard this hollow *boing-boing* sound. There was a pause and then the *boing-boing-boing* happened again. Strange, I thought.

The *boing-boing* repeated a third time, followed by a metallic thump. It sounded as if someone was shooting baskets. In addition to the hoops in the auditorium, there was an ancient basketball hoop in this courtyard that no one, as far as I remember, had ever used. It didn't even have a rope netting, it was so old. But who was shooting baskets now?

Curiosity killed the cat, but that bit of folk wisdom didn't stop me. I leaned forward and gently pushed some evergreen branches aside. All I could see was that the person was wearing a long, flowing black robe. A *nun* shooting baskets?

This was so odd, I had to see which nun it was. I leaned forward some more. I took a step, then another, and stuck my head out even farther. What I saw was a nun taking a really lame two-handed, flat-footed shot that missed the rusted hoop completely.

I took another tentative step forward to get a better view. The crack from something I stepped on caused the *boing-boing* to stop cold.

"Who's there?" asked an all-too-familiar voice. There was a pause. "I know someone is there, so please come out now."

There was no mistaking it. I was caught and trapped. I stepped out from behind the pine tree and said, "Um, it's only me, Sister."

"Master Murphy?" Sister Angelica Rose stood there in the middle of the courtyard clutching a basketball and looking completely baffled. "Why were you hiding there?"

"Um . . ." I wanted to buy time to think up a good response, but instead I blurted out, "I came out because it was hot inside and then I heard the convent door open and I got scared, so I hid there." I gestured toward the trees. Well, it was sort of true, so that might make it less of a sin.

There was an awkward pause as Sister Angelica studied me. She didn't look happy, but she didn't look absolutely annoyed, either. And trust me, I knew what her absolutely annoyed look looked like.

Then, out of nowhere, she said, "I'm considering starting a girls' basketball club next year. After Christmas vacation. But I don't know much about basketball." Another pause. "Do you know how to play basketball?"

Now, this question came as a complete surprise. It almost sounded as if she were asking for my help. "Um, a little."

"Did you see me shoot?" she asked.

"A little." You have to admit I had a way with words, especially when faced with what might turn out to be a fatal encounter.

She gave me a look that suggested I needed to say more. "And?"

"Well," I began, "you pushed the ball two-handed. Like a girl. And you are a girl, I guess, but . . . but that's not how you should shoot a basket. And you didn't really jump. I mean, it's called a jump shot, and you're supposed to, um, you know, jump when you shoot."

On top of the weirdness of a nun shooting baskets, here I was explaining a jump shot — one hand guides the ball while the other pushes it toward the basket, and you actually get on your toes and jump —even though I wasn't very good at basketball. Iggy, Squints, Tom-Tom, and Mayor were way better than me. But for my survival I thought I should offer some help. Maybe it would become the first positive comment ever in my red folder.

But I was squirming. I wanted to be away from Sister Angelica and this basketball lesson.

Angelica took a few shots, and all of them fell way short. She was pushing the ball off better, but she never actually got off her feet. She looked as if she weighed a thousand pounds and was glued to the ground.

Then my brain took over again, and I was remembering the red folder incident, being sent to the back of the class and embarrassed in front of Kathy Gathers, ending up as the Green Banana, having to rewrite a silly thank-you letter over and over again, and how she humiliated Philip. And feeling increasingly annoyed. No, angry. So angry it felt as if my brain had expanded and was pressing against the inside of my skull. I told you before that my brain jumped around for no reason and got me into trouble.

Angelica bounced the ball several times, then stared at the rusty hoop, raised the ball, and . . . and

. . . I exploded. "For God's sake, JUMP!!!!" I screamed. And she did.

You never raise your voice to a nun. That's an unwritten rule everyone knows. And here I was, angry and yelling at her *and* bringing God into it, too. I was going to hell, no doubt about it. But Sister Angelica did manage to launch the ball in a high arc, and it sailed toward the hoop.

And go figure, it went through without touching iron. No sound whatsoever. A perfect shot.

The ball hit the pavement and went *boing-boing-boing* as it bounced along. Angelica didn't say a thing. I didn't say a thing.

Then she did one of the nastiest, cruelest things she had done to me all year. She turned, looked me square in the eyes, and smiled.

21
Now What?

A SMILE IS a good thing, I'm told. It suggests that the smiler is friendly and reasonably happy. A smile is cost-free and doesn't require a lot of work or muscle power, and it means the receiver of the smile probably won't be hit anytime soon. All good. So why did I find Angelica's smile so cruel and nasty?

She'd never actually smiled in class that I could remember. Certainly not in my direction. Plus that cardboard coif thing she wore made her look pinched and crabby and old. Not Sister Immaculata ancient old, but oldish.

The smile changed her face entirely. The lines near her eyes and the sides of her mouth vanished. Her eyes actually seemed to sparkle with fun. Fun! She looked a lot younger, too. In fact, she suddenly seemed not much older than the high school girls I passed on the way home.

And this is why that smile was an especially bad thing. When I thought about the high school girls, I wondered if Sister Angelica had ever worn a short plaid skirt and tight sweater. And what she might look like in them. And this prompted an image of Sister Angelica dressed in such an outfit to flash in my noodle.

I would have put exclamation points at the end of that last sentence, but they would have had to take up at least ten pages of this book. The image was in my mind for only a second or two—like a mortar explosion—but believe me, it made my brain scream and go blank. Thinking it, seeing it, remembering it was definitely a major-league sin, and I was sure that a dark, avenging cloud would appear above me and that the Almighty Himself would emerge and cleave me top to bottom with some sort of wicked-looking ax. I waited to hear the rumble of thunder that would announce the cloud's arrival.

Then my brain began to clear, and all I was facing was Angelica and she was still smiling. Then her expression changed. "Is everything all right, James?"

"Ah, yeah. I mean, yes, Sister." Actually, since the cloud hadn't appeared and I was still alive, I had started wondering what my red folder would look like after the addition of "he screamed at me using God's name in vain" and "he imagined me in a plaid skirt and tight sweater." I assumed she would know about the outfit thought through cosmic nun power.

"Good. You looked distressed." She turned to face the hoop, picked up the ball, and made ready to shoot again. "So I guide the ball with one hand, shoot with the other, and jump when I do that."

I didn't say a thing.

She jumped and launched the ball in a high arc. This time the ball hit the front lip of the rim, bounced off the backboard, landed on the side of the rim, and started rolling around. When it slowed enough, it fell in. She retrieved the ball and came back to shoot again with a very satisfied look on her face.

"Is there anything else that might help me shoot better?" she asked, facing away from me as she set up for her next shot.

"Yes. Wear sneakers." Which was true. She and every other nun wore these clunky sensible black shoes with a little heel. But as soon as it was out of my mouth, I had a feeling it sounded sarcastic, so I rushed to make it good. "You can get black high-top sneakers, so no one would know you had them on."

She laughed a little (also a first this year), jumped, and shot. This time the ball hit the rim and bounced off.

"Hmmm," she said. "I prefer red."

Red? I thought. Red high-tops? Now *that* was a surprise, but maybe not any more than a nun shooting baskets and bowling.

She took several more shots. Some went in, some didn't. And I offered bits of advice, such as reminding her to shoot the ball in a nice high arc.

Suddenly she tucked the ball under her arm and spun to face me. "I have an idea, James," she said, looking serious. "I'm going to try to start a girls' basketball league in the auditorium next February. Maybe you could come by and give us some pointers. Like the ones you gave me today. What do you think?"

She said this in a perfectly nice way, mind you. It was a real question, not a question that was a command. But it made me very nervous anyway. Things hadn't gone too well in the classroom so far this year, and you never know what might happen after school out in the open auditorium. I think I hemmed and hawed a few seconds before an idea came to me. "I'm actually not very good at basketball. I don't even know much about the game." She looked disappointed, so I tossed in "But Mayor and Iggy and Tom-Tom and Squints are pretty good."

She blinked and looked baffled. "Iggy, Tom-Tom, and Squints?" I told her who they were. "Oh," she said. "So do you think they might help us a little? And you, too?"

Now I had done it. To get out of being a target, I'd made them targets. And I hadn't even escaped! "I don't know. I guess I could ask them."

"Tell them it would be a big help. It won't start for a while, so they have time to think it over, and tell them it won't take up much time. Fifteen or so minutes maybe twice a week. Mr. Bernie is going to try to get nets for those old hoops."

"Um, okay."

"Oh, and perhaps Philip might be able to join us. I think speaking English more might help him. I've been reading about . . ." She didn't seem to want to say the word "stuttering." "Well, some people say that more opportunities to speak can help. Could you ask him, too?"

"Um, well, I guess." I am nothing if not a genius in conversation.

"Thank you, James." She glanced at her watch. "Lunch period is almost over, so you might want to go inside and eat."

I needed urgently to get to the auditorium, where the triggering device was being set up. I knew the guys would be disappointed, but now Sister Angelica had actually been nice to me and gotten me to volunteer to coach her basketball league. And then there was Kathy. I had to stop the flour-ball-in-the-stomach explosion.

I had intended to go in through the door closest to the auditorium, but with Sister Angelica still out in the courtyard, that was out of the question. A new route suddenly occurred to me. I headed back to the door I'd just come out of. I wouldn't go to the cafeteria — I would take the long way around, past Sister Rose Mary's office, down the hallway filled with windows and the long dark hallways, to the back stairs. I could run part of the way, so it might not take long.

I went inside, but instead of heading down toward the cafeteria, I took a step up toward the first floor and Sister Rose Mary's office. Suddenly a giant dark shadow blocked the light and my path. I glanced up and up and up at what might have been a hundred-story black skyscraper named Sister Rose Vincent.

"And where do you think you're going?" she demanded.

"Um . . ." This was one time I was thankful for my bulging red MURPHY folder. "I have to go to Sister Rose Mary's," I said with great confidence, maybe even pride. No one could possibly question this, not with my track record so carefully written down. I grabbed the handrail, pulled myself up a step, and tried to slither past her.

Sister Rose Vincent tossed a hip left to block my way. "Not so fast," she said. "Sister Rose Mary isn't in her office right now."

"Oh. Well, I can go and wait for her." Again, I made a move to get past her, but she didn't budge.

"She won't be back for some time. You should go to the cafeteria and wait for the bell. And no dawdling."

"Yes, Sister."

I turned and went downstairs, one slow, sad step at a time. My mind was racing, trying to work out a new plan. But all I heard inside my head was *Now what?*

22

Nella Bocca del Lupo

TWO HOURS LATER I was backstage with all the second graders. The first graders were singing and dancing their hearts out, which meant the second graders were on next. *I* would be on next.

Our group was standing to the side and unnaturally quiet, probably because everyone was nervous. The auditorium was packed with kids, all of them following every move taking place onstage. Bernie had tried to get the curtain to work, but it jammed, so it would stay open for today's show. I heard one Yellow Banana say he wasn't sure he would remember the dance steps. Another hoped she wouldn't forget the words to the song. Which Sister Mary Brian finally had given them a few days before, saying she was sorry, but she was able to think up only one verse.

I was nervous too, not so much about remembering the words. I was nervous thinking about the exploding flour ball and wondering if it really had been hooked up. There had been a lot of last-minute clearing out and moving of things in the auditorium, plus setting up the folding chairs, so the guys hadn't gotten back to class in time to tell me what had or had not happened.

After I put on my costume, I squinted to focus my eyes and stared hard at the alleys. This wasn't easy to do through my costume porthole. The yellow police line and corner posts had been removed, so nothing blocked my vision. Still, I couldn't see the fishing line, either at the beginning of the gleaming alleys or at the spot where the line was supposed to lead up to the hanging ball. I leaned over, stared so hard my eyes hurt, then looked up at the ball and tried to follow where the line should come down. If it was hooked up, the black paint had made it disappear.

I was about to give up when I noticed the slightest bit of a flash, a paper-thin two-inch-long line of reflected light hovering halfway between the floor and the ceiling. So it was hooked up and ready to go. Okay, now what was I going to do?

"Are you looking at something?" one of the Yellow Bananas asked in a whisper.

"No," I replied softly, straightening up and trying to look innocent.

"I saw you too. You were looking at something," said another Yellow Banana. "What is it?" He looked down the alley and said to a third banana, "The Green Banana saw something over there, but I can't see it. Can you?"

Sister Mary Brian saved me from having the entire Victory-V of Yellow Bananas checking to see what I had been looking at. She quieted the chatter and told us to get ready. So much for my plausible deniability. "Break a leg, everybody," she added as she left the stage for the piano. I knew from the back of the *Language Arts* book that that was a way to wish performers good luck before they went on, but it still seemed like a wish for bad luck.

The first grade finished up to lots of applause and several loud whistles. Patrolling nuns quickly silenced the whistling offenders. Then it was the second graders' turn.

The Banana Boat group went first, followed by the Rhyming Bananas. This second song was pretty lively.

The kids seemed to have a lot of fun performing, and they got the loudest applause — along with whistles from some foolishly brave kids, several of whom were escorted from the auditorium.

After the Rhyming Bananas had taken their bows and exited the stage, the Yellow Bananas and I went to our positions. I had to hop-waddle onto the stage, and even though I was as graceful as possible, there was still a smattering of laughter from the audience. By this time I was sweating like crazy and trying to suck in air. I was nervous about being in front of the entire school and also about the booby trap just behind me.

I could hear some of the Yellow Bananas still worrying out loud. I was worrying too, about everything. Especially whether I would survive the afternoon. All my nervousness disappeared when Sister Mary Brian called out, "And one . . . and two . . . and THREE!" And she hit those piano keys like a ton of bricks.

The plan for our routine was simple. Sister Mary Brian would play the first two — I think she called them bars — of music and we wouldn't move at all. Then we would do two sets of box steps without singing. We would start singing during the next two sets of box steps while we all continued dancing. Because there was only one verse, we would sing that verse twice and then stop.

On cue, I stepped forward, my arms flapping this way and that to keep me balanced. I assumed that the Yellow Bananas, as instructed, were waving their arms a little bit so the audience would think my dancing style was planned. I heard a few kids in the audience start to laugh, and I began to sweat hard. I was afraid the entire mess would become a bad joke and Sister Mary Brian would be so embarrassed that she'd stop playing. But she thumped on in grand style.

I must have been distracted. As we finished our second non-singing box step, I leaned over too far and felt myself tipping off balance. To stop myself from toppling over, I had to fling my arms up, and I managed to do a complete one-footed spin. A second later the audience roared with laughter, and some even applauded, and I realized that all the Yellow Bananas must have followed my lead.

No time to stop, since Sister Mary Brian sure wasn't stopping. So, as directed, I stepped off into the next box step, and the Victory-V burst into song:

> "Heeeee's . . . a big green banana
> and he's sad, sad, sad.

He wants to go home
in your grocery bag.
Heeeeee . . . wants to be yellow,
he wants to be sweet.
He wants to be loved
just like your ground meat."

I have to admit, I was glad Sister Mary Brian had run out of creative energy—who knows what a second verse would have said. We kept on dancing and repeating the lyrics until Sister Mary Brian—with gusto—came to a thunderous ending. And the auditorium went wild.

No, really. They were clapping and shouting and whistling. Our instructions were to stop, do a little bow, and then stand there quietly while Sister Angelica came onstage and delivered her message. Sister Mary Brian came bounding up first. "Excellent. Excellent," she said with real enthusiasm. I couldn't see her through my tiny porthole, but from the sound of her voice I figured that she turned to face the audience. "Everyone. Everyone. I need your attention, please."

Patrolling nuns began hushing the audience, and soon the auditorium became deadly quiet. It happened so quickly it was actually a little spooky. Sister Mary

Brian continued. "Sister Angelica Rose has a couple of very important announcements to make, and I hope we will all give her our full attention."

A moment later Sister Angelica walked quickly past my line of vision, followed by someone a little shorter, obviously a student. I swiveled a tad and almost said something out loud when I saw Kathy Gathers standing beside Sister Angelica.

Sister Angelica began explaining about the bowling alleys and how Bernie had worked so hard to restore them. And Bernie got his own round of applause, which was nice. Then she continued her announcement. But I wasn't really taking much of it in. My brain was churning through why Kathy Gathers was up on the stage with Sister Angelica Rose. I knew Kathy was one of the good-smart kids, but there were other good-smart kids, so why her?

". . . a girls' bowling league." There were some cheers for this, mostly from girls. A few boys called out, "What about us?" The cheers won out. Sister Angelica continued: "We'll be taking down names all next week, and we'll start the league the week after that. You'll be getting a note about this to show your parents."

Sister Angelica let a few moments go by as the audience settled down. "We have an even more important announcement to make today." She paused and put her hand on Kathy's shoulder. "Kathy's parents and all of us at St. Stephen's are so proud of her. After a great deal of discussion and thought and prayer, Kathy has decided that after she graduates from high school, she is going to become a postulant to the order of Sisters of Charity. Kathy has . . ."

Postulant? I'd heard the word before, but I wasn't sure what it meant. It sounded like a very bad, very gooey disease. Then it dawned on me, and my brain screamed: *What?!?!* Ten pages of exclamation points and question marks would not even begin to show you what I felt at that instant. One hundred pages wouldn't do it. Plus my brain finally did short-circuit in a light show of colors and fireworks and internal screams and wails.

I was so stunned I stumbled back until some Yellow Bananas stopped me. Kathy Gathers — my Kathy Gathers — was going to become a nun. Forever. My dreams for the future — our future together — were shattered, over, dead, gone, destroyed, obliterated . . .

". . . and as a special honor to Kathy, she will throw the first ball on our newly redone bowling alleys."

This produced another *What?!?!* I was trying to organize my thoughts in some sort of rational way, and that was the best my brain could come up with. Meanwhile, Sister Mary Brian ghosted up from backstage and handed Kathy a shiny black bowling ball. Kathy took it, turned, and made a step toward the alley.

Having the exploding flour ball hit Sister Angelica would be bad enough, but if it hit Kathy . . . I couldn't begin to imagine how bad things would be. So I did the only thing I could do. I went into action.

I threw myself into a spinning turn, pushed a Yellow Banana aside, and went fat duck hop-waddling toward the alley. I got there a few steps before Kathy, slid across the black foul line, and felt the tripwire jam my foot. I looked up.

There is slow. And there is slow motion. I felt as if I had been standing there for several minutes with nothing happening. The triggering device hadn't worked, and I had just made a fool of myself for no—

And then it was there, the bag, sailing in the planned arc and headed directly for me. It happened so fast I couldn't move before the bag hit me right square in the porthole.

All I knew was that the inside of the Green Banana costume filled with billowing flour dust, and I started coughing. Meanwhile, outside, there was another explosion—of gasps, shouts, cheers, a chorus of coughing (I assume from a spreading cloud of flour dust), and one voice from nearby — I think it was Al the Second Grader — proclaiming, "That was so cool!" I did what any right-thinking kid would do: I ran.

Or rather, I started hop-waddling to escape what would surely be the most horrible punishment since the Spanish Inquisition. I cut across the stage — hop-waddle, hop-waddle — headed for the door to the stairway. Through the door — hop-waddle, hop-waddle — to the stairs, then up.

This might sound easy, but it wasn't, trust me. Hop-waddling up stairs doesn't work. I had to grab both handrails and haul myself up two or three steps at a time. A moment later I burst out the side door, slid down the banister to the courtyard pavement, and hop-waddled my way up the side walkway of the convent to Beech Street. Then I hop-waddled toward the end of the street.

By this time, I had come up with a plan, a feeble one at best. Beech was a dead end, but there was an opening in the fence that led to what we called "the cut," a dirt path that paralleled the train tracks and emptied onto Kearny Avenue. And freedom.

I had almost reached the end of the street when I realized my escape plan's fatal flaw. The opening in the fence wasn't very big, just big enough for a kid to squeeze through, and I still had on my seven-foot-tall banana costume, with no way to unzip and get out of it. So I stopped hop-waddling.

I was exhausted, and wisps of flour dust still clouded up the inside of the costume. I stood there panting like a dog in July and leaned over to see if that would help me breathe better. That's when I noticed I was standing next to a bench, where Sister Immaculata was sitting, staring up at me.

"Good . . . afternoon . . .Sister," I panted as politely as possible. I saw dust swirls drifting over Sister Immaculata.

And do you know what she did? She started laughing. I mean, everybody always laughed at me, but a nun! Her laugh was a cross between a cackle and a giggle, and it seemed to echo in the street.

Because I'd been laughed at before, I knew this wasn't a mean cackle-giggle. In fact she seemed to be really enjoying herself. I could tell when she stopped saying her rosary, dropped the beads into her lap, and pointed at me, cackle-giggling even harder.

After a while she settled down and must have heard me wheezing. She patted the place next to her and suggested that I sit down. I plopped down beside her, which was not easy to do in a stiff, oddly shaped banana costume.

She chuckle-giggled a little more, then asked, "What's your name?" Her voice was shaky and a little raspy.

Because of the costume, I was sitting straight up and facing forward, so I was looking directly across the street. To talk to her I had to lean over, and the top of my banana costume nearly hit her in the head.

"James Murphy," I told her.

"James Murphy," she said thoughtfully. She repeated the name softly a couple of times. "I had a James Murphy in class long ago. Are you related to him?"

"He's my dad, Sister."

She cackle-giggled a few times, then said, "Well, that explains it. He was quite a scamp, too, when he was here. Always up to something. Has he done okay? You know, we were all worried about him."

"He's done okay," I said. I was puzzled because I'd never, ever heard that my father had a scamp side. I wondered if he and my mom had other secrets and how I could find out about them. "He's a certified public accountant," I added proudly.

"Good, good," she said. "You tell him Sister

Immaculata says hello. And tell him I still remember the eraser incident. That had us puzzled for days."

"The eraser incident?" I wanted to know what he'd done that had stuck in Sister Immaculata's memory for decades.

"It turned out to be very funny," she said. "You should ask him. I think you and your father have a lot in common, judging by that costume." She cackle-giggled some more.

Just then I heard my name called, and Vero and Philip came running up.

"You need to come back, Murph," Vero said. "Now."

Sister Immaculata patted my hand and said, "You run along now. And remember to say hello for me."

"I will, Sister."

Vero and Philip hauled me to my feet. I asked them to unzip me so I could walk back like a human, but the zipper was stuck and wouldn't budge. So they walked and I hop-waddled.

"We're cooked," Vero said. "They know everything."

"Everything?" I squeaked.

"Nella bocca del lupo," Philip said, shaking his head mournfully from side to side. In a soft, doomed voice he repeated, *"Nella bocca del lupo."*

23

And Everything in Between

"INTO THE MOUTH of the wolf" is what Philip had said, and he wasn't kidding. Philip and Vero had been ordered to fetch me and go directly to Sister Rose Mary's office. And no dawdling. When we got there, Mayor, Iggy, and Tom-Tom were standing in the middle of the room, looking nervous. Squints was nowhere to be seen, but no one blamed him for lying low.

When I tripped the exploding flour ball and hop-waddled off, it was clear that I was guilty. Sister Rose Mary had swooped into the aisle where the guys were sitting and poked her pirate hand into Mayor's chest. "Did you know about this, Master Mayor?" And Mayor, cornered, said yes immediately. Iggy was next to Mayor, and when poked, he also said he knew. Tom-Tom didn't even have to answer. When he lowered his head, he more than admitted to being a part of the plot. Philip and Vero confessed next and were sent to get me. The rest were sent to Sister Rose Mary's office and told to wait. As Mayor said with a certain degree of admiration, "She was quick and efficient and got the job done." Like a good insurance man, I figured.

We had to stand there and wait while the other grades did their performances. Mrs. Branfurs tried to unzip me from my banana costume, but she couldn't budge the zipper an inch. I was trapped in more ways than one.

After the first few minutes we were all pretty quiet, which let my brain bounce around from thought to thought until it stopped at Kathy Gathers. She was going to be a nun, and that meant she would be out of my life. Forever. I already felt my KG tattoo fading away.

Finally, Sister Rose Mary and Sister Angelica came in and confronted us.

"Why in heaven's name are you still wearing that ridiculous outfit?" Sister Rose Mary demanded. Fortunately, Mrs. Branfurs came to my defense by explaining that the zipper was stuck, but she wondered if maybe Bernie could get it open with a pair of pliers.

Then Sister Rose Mary got to the point. "Master

Murphy," she said, "why did you pull this . . . this . . . stunt?"

I have to admit I was a little hurt by her calling the costume ridiculous. It was, but I wasn't sure she should have made fun of Mr. Danes's hard work like that.

"We . . . I thought it would be fun, Sister."

"Fun! Someone might have gotten hurt. You do understand that?"

Here's the thing. I was trapped inside my costume, but also in a weird way protected by it. Like having a shield. So I actually said, "Well, *now* I do, Sister. I thought it would be something . . . I don't know. Unusual."

"Unusual!" And, like Erin (Margaret) O'Connor, Sister Rose Mary was off to the races — lecturing us about responsibility, putting innocent people in danger, creating a mess, and much, much more. Only when she said, "And you did all this as a practical joke!" did I realize that she didn't know it had been intended to murderlate-embarrass Sister Angelica. None of us corrected her. I once heard Uncle Arthur say, "A witness should only answer the question asked and should never volunteer additional information." Which sounded like good legal advice right now.

Sister Angelica added some words of her own — about how it didn't reflect well on her or Sister Mary Brian or the school — but she seemed more sad than angry. This entire episode was certainly going to make for interesting reading in my red MURPHY folder.

In the end, we were all ordered to march to the auditorium to help Bernie clean up the flour onstage and straighten up the place. We also had to help him with various other school things every day after class for two weeks, and we were told that a note would be sent home to our parents. All of which seemed like a pretty light sentence, considering.

And that was it. We did our Bernie time, which was a lot less painful than clock-watch time. The note sent home just said I would be helping Bernie organize the auditorium and other parts of the school. Sister Rose Mary didn't include any details about why we were helping, and I figured she didn't want to advertise the prank. My mom said, "Doing volunteer work will build your character."

I asked my dad about the eraser incident, and he told me about using egg whites to glue every blackboard eraser in his classroom to another one, eraser to eraser, so they stuck together. It didn't exactly sound like a prank to remember decades later, but maybe you had to be there.

Ellen McDonald kept after me about homework every single day for the rest of the school year. And over the following months my grades did improve. As I said once before, miracles do happen. I started to get between 75s and 80s. Not Roger Sutternhopf grade level, but not horrible, either.

One day in the spring we took a math test and scored each other's papers. I thought I'd done okay —Ellen had really drilled me on this section of the textbook—but I was still nervous when the scores were read aloud. At last Ruth Wisnewski stood and announced, "James Murphy," then said, "one hundred!"

I was stunned. A 30 was bad, but 100 percent incorrect was mind-bogglingly awful. Then it dawned on me what she really meant. The next second, the entire class started cheering, and I have to admit, it felt really good to be perfect for once. Sister Angelica might even have cracked a smile. A little one, but I'd take what I could get. Okay, not everyone was cheering. Roger had turned in his seat and was glowering at me. He only got a 90.

Naturally, my brain did its best to help me add to my red folder. A few weeks after the math test, Sister Angelica told us to write a brief essay on any subject in the science book, and we could consult the book while writing it. She wanted us to learn to be "concise and to the point," and she said that the shortest essay would earn an additional ten points.

I wanted those ten points, so I really thought about it, and without even consulting the text I wrote:

What a Nose Is Good For
A nose is good for smelling the roses and the garbage. A nose is good for breathing in air so you don't die. A nose is good for storing snot while you look for a Kleenex.
The End.

I thought adding "The End" made the whole thing seem pretty classy. Sister Angelica didn't, it seemed. I passed, but only because I had the shortest essay.

The bowling league was organized as planned, with five teams of six girls from a number of grades. Sister Angelica promised that next year there would also be a boys' team. When the bowling season ended in February, Sister Angelica announced the basketball league, which only fifteen girls signed up for. The guys did help out and had fun making believe they were NBA coaches and showing off for the girls.

And that's pretty much how the rest of the year went. No big mistakes (on my part), just working along day to day and trying not to get into trouble (not always successfully).

On the very last day of the school year, with summer vacation just seven minutes away, Sister Angelica said she wanted to make an announcement. The usual groans followed, of course, but she ignored them. "I think it's honest to say that we all had a very, very interesting year," she said. She may have glanced in my direction. "I know *I* have. And I think you've all learned a great deal, and you're ready for seventh grade. Now go home and have some fun." This resulted in an unorganized scramble for the door (the first of the year). Sister Angelica called out, "No running, please." And because it was impossible to escape without additional comment, she added, "And don't forget to read the books on the summer reading list."

As we approached the front door of the building, the entire herd of kids slowed. Sister Rose Vincent was standing there, her arms folded across her chest, looking sour and magically keeping everyone from rushing. I wondered if some cherry Jell-O might brighten her day.

A moment later I burst out of the school and into the warm sunshine. Free, I thought. For the next couple of months I'm completely, totally . . .

"Jimmy," a voice called. "Wait up, Jimmy." Ellen was right behind me. "I'm glad I caught up with you so we can talk about next week."

"Next week?"

"Yes. I'll call you on Monday night at seven. We can arrange to meet to go the library on Tuesday. Okay?"

"Well, no, now that you ask."

"Jimmy, you need to read the books on the list to be ready for seventh grade. You do have your list, right?"

"Yeah, I guess." We'd been given the usual wad of multicolored papers to bring home, and I assumed it might be in there somewhere.

"You guess? See, you need help to be sure you get it done. Otherwise you'll spend the entire summer playing baseball."

What was wrong with that, I wondered. "I think I can do it myself, Ellen. But thanks."

"Jimmy, I didn't work with you all year just to watch you fall behind again. I'll call you on Monday and we'll go to the library on Tuesday. You'll be done by noon, and then you can play your precious baseball." She looked me square in the eyes and smiled.

Back in September I would have given anything to have Kathy Gathers smile at me. But now Ellen was smiling, and nothing else really mattered.

Ellen didn't wait to see if I had an answer. She had turned and headed home, but I managed to call after her, "Okay, Monday." And it kind of felt good to have that on my schedule.

The guys had already split up and disappeared, so I bought some salty potato sticks and began striding home, munching as I went. On the way I passed the three high school girls, and as they glided past, Mr. MacGullion's daughter said, "Hey, Jim Murphy Jr. We'll see you next year, right?"

"Absolutely." I was oddly cheerful, I realized. Being out of school for the summer was one reason, but not even that would make me this strangely happy.

"You have a good summer, Jim Murphy Jr."

"I will," I answered. I took a step, then did a fast spin that was more graceful than my Green Banana spin onstage. "You, too." The quick wave of her hand told me she'd heard me.

Then I was hurrying along again. I had to talk to someone, to empty my brain of everything that was bouncing around in it now. When I pushed open the door to our house, I felt a cool calmness take hold of me. Even the new bright blue tiles in the kitchen made me happy. I checked from the kitchen and saw that Philip's light was on. I grabbed two bottles of Pepsi from the refrigerator and went out back to Philip's window.

Philip was reading a book of French phrases when I asked if he wanted a Pepsi. His screen slid up, and he took the bottle.

Here's the thing: I came to sixth grade hoping that I could change. And I did. But I realized that hoping and changing didn't just happen in an instant. It was everything between September and now that made the real difference. And I started reciting out loud what had happened to me that year.

"There was that first day with my red folder being waved in my face and Sister Angelica making you talk in English and me being embarrassed in front of Kathy Gathers. Then Sister Regina and that wormy chicken cutlet and Rose Vincent and Sister Rose Mary and clock-watch time. Getting a thirty percent on a quiz and having to call Ellen every night, hitting the door with my head and knocking Sister Ursula on her butt, getting sent to the Enforcer and becoming the Green Banana and having to write that thank-you letter over and over, and you having to stand up and read extra-credit words in English, me hiding behind Joey Spano and the cherry Jell-O incident. And the Plan . . . coming up with the Plan and how you guys volunteered to help Bernie to get it set up. And finding Sister Angelica shooting baskets and ending up helping her with the basketball team and imagining her wearing a short plaid skirt and tight sweater" — this was the only time Philip interrupted me with a "Huh?" so I explained quickly and went on — "then trying to stop the whole thing only to have Rose Vincent stop me, and singing and dancing in front of the entire school and Kathy Gathers becoming a nun and the flour ball exploding and me running and then meeting Sister Immaculata, Ellen and . . . and . . . and . . . everything else that happened."

When I stopped, I felt lightheaded and wondered how Erin (Margaret) could do this over and over again without fainting. All I could add was, "It was one weird year, Philip. One very weird year."

Philip stretched his Pepsi bottle out the window so he could clink the bottom with mine. Then he said clearly and confidently in what sounded like a completely new language for him, "Well, Murph, all's well that ends well."

What Philip Really Said

MY EDITOR WANTED ME to translate everything Philip said right in the text, but I said no. Philip hardly ever translated for us, and I figure that all of you are capable of looking back here at the translations if you feel like it. By the way, when I wrote to my editor to say no in-text translations, I ended my short message with something Philip once said: *"Quando si sottovalutano i vostri figli, voi sottovalutate voi stessi."* Something to think about, don't you agree?

CAVEAT EMPTOR: *Let the buyer beware. (Latin)*

ERIN GO BRAGH: *Ireland forever*

HOSTIS HUMANI GENERIS: *Enemy of the human race (Latin)*

MI NOMBRE ES . . . : *My name is . . . (Spanish)*

OBIT ANUS, ABIT ONUS: *The old woman dies, the burden is lifted. (Latin)*

IL TIRANNO SARA ROVESCIATE DA MANI DI MOLTE PERSONE BUONE: *The tyrant can be toppled by the hands of many good people. (Italian)*

ALEA IACTA EST: *The die is cast. (Latin)*

NON C'È NULLA DA TEMERE QUANDO GLI AMICI SONO VICINO: *There is nothing to fear when friends are near. (Italian)*

RINGRAZIO, IL MIO BUON AMICO. TI RINGRAZIO: *Thank you, my good friend. Thank you. (Italian)*

J'ACCUSE: *I accuse. (French)*

NELLA BOCCA DEL LUPO: *Into the mouth of the wolf (Italian)*

QUANDO SI SOTTOVALUTATE I VOSTRI FIGLI, VOI SOTTOVALUTATE VOI STESSI: *When you underestimate your children, you underestimate yourself. (Italian)*

SEMPRE LA VERITÀ FA MALE IL COLPEVOLE: *The truth always hurts the guilty. (Italian)*